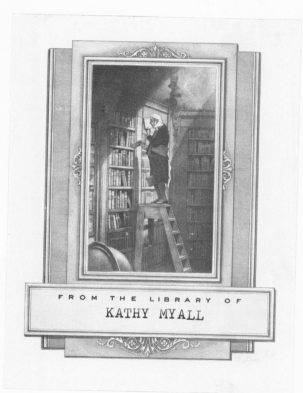

PRISONER
OF
THE QUEEN

Also by
Alison Macleod

THE HERETIC

THE HIRELING

CITY OF LIGHT

THE MUSCOVITE

ALISON MACLEOD

PRISONER
OF
THE QUEEN

Boston

HOUGHTON MIFFLIN COMPANY

1973

First printing c

First American Edition 1973
Copyright © 1972 by Alison Macleod.
All rights reserved. No part of this work
may be reproduced or transmitted in any
form by any means, electronic or mechanical,
including photocopying and recording,
or by any information storage or retrieval
system, without permission in writing
from the publisher.
ISBN: 0-395-14010-2
Library of Congress Catalog Card Number: 72-9077
Printed in the United States of America

To
Dudley White

I

OUR LOVE AND REVERENCE for Father Possevino made us very willing to obey his messenger. Yet we found some of the instructions curious. It was not enough that we should make our guest-rooms fit for the envoys of an emperor. We had also to warn two other religious houses — there were only two, besides our own, in Brno—to make their best rooms ready. Not that these Russians were numerous. Besides the ambassador there were only six noblemen, the messenger said, and some servants. But they quarrelled so much that Father Possevino did not believe he could bring them all to Rome alive, unless he kept them separate on the journey.

"Well, yes, barbarians!" the messenger agreed. "Very pious, though, in their own heretic way. Father Possevino has good hopes of winning them back to the Church. Only he's afraid they may be horrified by what they see in Rome."

We were interrupted by the voice of our novice-master, who had come among us, as usual, silently. He said: "Rome has changed under the influence of our Society. There is no excuse now for the heretics to complain."

The messenger faltered. He was a mere novice like ourselves. "Father . . . Reverend Father, it is not only Rome. They may take exception even to what they see here."

"I cannot answer for the other monasteries," our novice-master said. "Our Society lives by its rules."

"Father Possevino knows that," the novice assured him. "But if you have any more pictures like . . . well, like that one . . ."

The Italian picture in our entrance hall showed Mary Magdalen washing the feet of Christ. Our Father Superior, who now joined us, pointed out that the Magdalen was modestly dressed.

The novice, looking at the ground, said: "Yes, but she is visibly a woman. To the Russians that means the painting is not religious. And our statues of angels offend them, if the angels are showing their legs. And sometimes, in this hot weather, when the novices chop wood, they take off their habits and work in a loincloth. The Russians cannot bear that. They think it as immodest for a man to bare his breast as for a woman."

"We shall cover up our paintings, our statues and ourselves," replied the Father Superior. "What else does Father Possevino advise?"

"Father Possevino has grown a beard. The Russians think that a man who shaves is defacing the image of God. They will be here this time tomorrow, and of course you cannot grow beards by then. But if those who have beards already could be conspicuous . . ."

Our superior, who was clean-shaven, smiled and turned to me. "You must put yourself well forward, Paul. That great yellow bush of yours will please them."

He then enquired how we were to talk to our guests. All this conversation had been in Italian, which we used among ourselves, because we had all been educated in Rome. But in our present work of converting the heretic peasants round Brno, we had learned Bohemian. Was it true, asked the Father Superior, that this was akin to Russian?

8

"It is not very like," said the novice. "But the Russians will understand you, if you tell them they are welcome."

My part in the welcome was to help the choirmaster. The Bohemians have songs whose tunes are very beautiful, though the words are worldly or heretic. Since I first began to learn their language, I had been fitting Catholic words to these tunes. Now my superiors often told me to sing them, sometimes with the choir and sometimes alone. Though I was twenty-two I could still sing almost as high as a boy.

So I stood in the first rank of the choir, outside the main gate of our House, waiting for the Russians.

We knew when they were coming because the guard, posted on the walls of Brno, gave the signal to ring the church bells. The chief citizens rode out to escort the Russians; the common people poured into the streets. As the Russians approached our gate the bells fell silent, and so, suddenly, did the people. They could see us making ready to sing. Heretics to a man, they could not refrain from hearing the music of our Church.

Only the Russians gave no sign of pleasure. They showed no pain either; above their great brown beards, their eyes were narrow and wary.

Father Possevino smiled. We scarcely knew how to smile in return; we were so startled at the change in him. In six years he had become a haggard old man. His hair was thin, and the beard he had grown to please the Russians was grey. His eyes were very weary. Yet he smiled. With infinite grace and courtesy, he shepherded apart the four Russians who were to stay in the other monasteries.

Our part was to entertain the ambassador, Yakov Molvaninov, and two noblemen who were his particular friends. I sang to them again as they had supper. When I paused, Yakov Molvaninov beckoned to me. He wanted to stroke my beard. He invited the others to stroke it. I found I could understand a few words of what they said. "More like silk than hair!" "A gift of God!" I answered in Bohemian, and found that they caught a word or two.

At my ear Father Possevino murmured: "Entertain them for

a few minutes. I have to go and make sure that the others are comfortable."

The Russians were trying to teach me one of their songs. But they were too drunk to keep their voices together. Besides, they could not agree as to the tune. Soon they began to quarrel, and I heard more words I understood. Like the Bohemian peasants, these noblemen were accusing one another of incest.

I looked round for Father Possevino, but he had not yet returned. So I myself rebuked the Russians for using such words in a religious house. They were taken aback. They had not known, they said, that anyone could understand them. I said: "But God understands you!"

"True!" said Molvaninov. "True! God is a Russian."

Then they all in turn embraced me and begged my pardon. They stroked my beard, as if I were a cat to be smoothed down. I purred like a cat, and they laughed. Soon they let me and my companions help them to their feather beds.

I was now so weary that I could hardly walk towards my own straw pallet. I did not know if I had breath enough to say my evening prayers.

I was at the dormitory door when I was called back. The Father Superior wanted to see me.

It is miraculous what power God gives us to carry out our vow of obedience. My feet, which had scarcely been able to drag me along, moved lightly and swiftly to the Father Superior's room.

I found him talking to Father Possevino. They were old friends; they had studied together in Rome. Besides, Father Possevino had stayed with us for a month, snowbound, on his way to Sweden. That was six years ago, in 1577, and since then he had shown Europe what it meant to be a Jesuit. That he had won King John of Sweden back from the Lutheran heresy, that he had been chosen by King Stephan Batory of Poland to lead a mission of peace to the Tsar—this I knew, and was amazed to find this friend of great kings greeting me as a friend.

My superior told him my name, Paul Calverley.

"I remember," Father Possevino said. "You were a pupil of the other Englishman, Edmund Campion."

Being so tired, I could not stop the tears which prickled my eyes at that name. Father Possevino told me I ought to rejoice that Edmund Campion was a blessed saint in Heaven. I said my grief was not for the loss of my dear teacher, but that I had not been found worthy to share his martyrdom.

"You were too young to go to England then," said the Father Superior briskly. "You may be a martyr yet, but for the present I am sending you to Rome, with Father Possevino. I appoint him your superior."

I bowed. To thank the Father Superior for his orders would be almost as insolent as to question them. But Father Possevino thanked him. To me he said: "I hear you made up a quarrel between the Russians. You have pleasant manners. I suppose you are a gentleman?"

I told him that my mother and father were gentlefolk, and rich enough, once, to send me to Rome for my education. But they had since been ruined by the fines they paid for not attending the English church.

"With God's help, we shall regain England," Father Possevino said. "Look at Poland! It was almost a Protestant country, a few years ago. Look here in Bohemia — the first of all Protestant countries — how many new Catholic churches there are within ten miles of Brno! I believe we shall gain even Russia for the Faith. That's why I shall be glad of your help in bringing these Russians to Rome."

I said: "Father, I am afraid you may be disappointed in me. I can scarcely talk to the Russians."

"But I have just seen you, prattling away."

"I was prattling Bohemian. They may have understood one word in three."

"When I was asked to negotiate peace between Poland and Russia," Father Possevino said, "I knew not one word of either language."

"Didn't they understand Latin?" asked the Father Superior.

"A few Poles did — no Russians. There is a part of Poland

where the people speak Russian. King Stephan scoured the monasteries there; he found me a man who was a good Catholic, knew Latin, and had education enough to expound both state affairs and the mysteries of our Faith. So I had a good interpreter. But the Russians did not want to understand us. In Moscow the courtiers laughed at our plain black robes. Tsar Ivan seemed to grow deaf at the word *peace*. He did send some of his noblemen back to Poland with me. But he warned them not to concede an inch. And then, in Poland, I found the noblemen urging King Stephan not to make peace. Both sides had to go through another winter of war before I could persuade them to meet. Then they sat in their tent for weeks, choking over a word, a comma, while the soldiers of both armies were dying in their sight. At last I brought both Poles and Russians to sign, and found that I was only beginning my real work. The treaty, you see, had to be ratified in Moscow, and the question was who would venture to take it there. It was known by then that Tsar Ivan had killed his own son."

The Father Superior shuddered. "We have heard of this," he said. "I hoped it was a fable."

"No, it's true. In one of his drunken rages . . . I never saw the hand of God so plainly, as on my second visit to Moscow. The courtiers who had laughed at us for wearing black were all in black. There were black hangings on the palace walls. The Tsar himself was in black, bare-headed, his crown laid aside, his face gaunt with fasting. That man loved the son he killed. So I found him chastened, willing to sign the treaty, willing to listen while I expounded the Faith. He still would have it, though, that the Greek Church was best. He told me what he had heard against the Popes. The Borgia family . . . The sons called nephews . . . The whores riding in Cardinals' carriages . . ."

"But this is very familiar!" said the Father Superior. "We hear it from the Protestants every day. How could it have reached Russia?"

"Oh, through the English. The English merchants are all

great heretics, and they swagger about Moscow as if they owned it. They very nearly do. All the country's foreign trade is in their hands. And some of them are educated men; they spoke to me in Latin. They speak familiarly to the Tsar in his own language. In that court where everyone is terrified, they never show a tremor. If only one of them had been a Catholic, and my interpreter!"

The Father Superior broke in. "You said you had a good interpreter."

"Very good, until the moment when he lost his tongue. That was my fault. I allowed myself to be a little angry. When the Tsar brought out more and more of these old stories against the Pope, I said — I think too sharply — that His Holiness was nevertheless the successor of St. Peter. I asked the Tsar: 'Are you the lawful heir of Prince Vladimir, who ruled Muscovy five centuries ago?' He agreed he was. I said: 'Well, suppose that one of your subjects refused to obey you, because in your human frailty you had committed some crime . . .' At that Ivan, half-rising from his seat, declared: 'Your Roman pontiff is no shepherd; he's a wolf!' This was the moment when my poor interpreter became speechless with terror. I had to go on by myself. And, like this young man, I thought I did not know Russian. I thought all my efforts to learn it, until then, had been unavailing. Yet God opened my mouth and I heard myself utter the phrase: 'Pastor of the Church'. I reminded the Tsar that he had addressed the Pope in this way, thereby admitting that he was our shepherd. The Tsar stood up and waved at me a staff tipped with iron — the very staff that he had used to kill his son. He shouted: 'You have been teaching the peasants in the market place to insult me!' At that not only my interpreter was silent. Every soul in the court was silent. I heard them holding their breath. God gave me the power to smile and say: 'I know that I am talking to a good and prudent prince, whom I have served faithfully — as you have seen in the peace treaty — and for whom the Pope also feels a fatherly love . . .' Ivan sat down. The courtiers gasped. My interpreter recovered his wits."

The Father Superior turned to me. "You see what it means to be a Jesuit, Paul? You can overcome even mortal fear."

Father Possevino smiled. "Oh, I still felt afraid. The worst moment was two days afterwards, when the Tsar sent for me again. My companions and I gave one another the last rites. But – as this young man complains – I was not found worthy of martyrdom. God put the Tsar into such a good temper that he made me sit down with him. He apologised for insulting the Pope. 'Don't tell him what I said!' That was when he told me he was sending his ambassador to Rome with me. He hopes the Pope will send him soldiers against the heathen Tartars. Which I am sure his Holiness would gladly do, if the Russians would embrace the Faith."

The next day, before setting out with Father Possevino, I made my confession to the Father Superior. "At midnight," I told him, "when the bell rang for the examination of conscience I became aware that I had a sin of pride . . ."

Here I faltered, because it was so shameful. He prompted me. "You are proud that you have been chosen to go to Rome?"

"No, Reverend Father!" And in fact I felt no pride at that. I thought I had been chosen by mistake. "No, it's a worse kind of pride. When Father Possevino spoke of the English merchants in Moscow, there was a moment when I did not think of them as heretics, lost souls, the persecutors of good Catholics, the murderers of Edmund Campion. I felt proud of being English."

I knelt with head bowed, expecting the rebuke which I knew by heart. We Jesuits had no country, indeed no father and mother. Peter Faber, our Founder's companion, when he passed through his native town, had not slackened his pace to greet his own family. A Jesuit was a soldier of Christ, bound to serve in whatever place, amid whatever people, our General directed.

The Father Superior did say this, but rapidly. Then he added: "I observed last night, when you spoke of your family's misfortunes, you did not have the tone . . ." He paused. After a time I ventured to ask: "What tone, Reverend Father?"

"The grating tone of grievance. It would give you away, whatever disguise you wore. If it's gone . . . If you feel a softening in your heart, towards all Englishmen . . . Well! We shall miss you, Paul. We shall miss your voice in our choir."

For the journey he directed me to take the best horse. And as I mounted it he gave me a letter, to carry to the General of our order, Father Aquaviva, in Rome.

II

UNTIL I HAD MASTERED their language, I tried to entertain the Russians, by singing to them. They in turn taught me their songs, and so we passed pleasantly over the tedious parts of our journey.

The road was as easy as earthly powers could make it. The Emperor's troops escorted us into Prague; the Emperor himself made us welcome at Vienna. In Venice golden barges escorted us along the Grand Canal. One barge carried lute-players and singing boys. The sweet high notes told me I had returned into that sunny world which I had almost forgotten in the forests of Bohemia.

The Russians remarked that the choirs in their country were better, because they used the deep voices of grown men. On seeing the Doge's palace they said that their Tsar had many palaces, each one larger than this. Inside the palace, however, the banquet pleased them. The Doge had employed cooks from Spalato, who knew the favourite dishes of the Slavs.

Father Possevino showed a special pleasure in conversing with a nobleman, Giacomo Buoncompagno. I understood why.

His presence there showed how far our Church had been reformed. True, Signor Buoncompagno was the bastard son of the Pope. But, because of the Jesuits, the Pope had not been able to make him a cardinal, or even keep him in Rome. He might live as a nobleman only so long as he stayed in Venice.

After the banquet the Doge made a speech of welcome to the Russians, pausing while I translated. Then, speaking more rapidly, the Doge said that Venice had a special reason to thank Father Possevino. Some Venetian sailors had been captured by the Turks, and sold to the Crimean Tartars. As pack slaves, these Venetians were with a Tartar army which invaded Russia. During the fighting a dozen of them escaped, and wandered about that scarcely peopled country, living on what wild animals they could catch. When at last they came to a town, they showed the crosses marked on their skins, and the Russians fed them well, seeing that they were Christians. (All Italian sailors have crosses indelibly stained on their bodies. On whatever shore they are washed up, they may have Christian burial.) Tsar Ivan, when he heard of these foreigners, sent them to Vologda, because the town was full of Englishmen, and Ivan thought that all foreigners were much the same. In fact the English treated them kindly, and succeeded in making out who they were. It was about them that an English merchant had spoken in Latin to Father Possevino. He had arranged their journey back to Venice.

As the Doge concluded his speech, he gave the signal for the sailors themselves to enter. They were in their best clothes, but still it could be seen that they were very rough, salt-baked, sun-hardened men. It was all the more moving when they went down on their knees to Father Possevino. They offered him a gold chain—a delicate model of the chains they had worn as prisoners. He directed them to give it to the Russian ambassador, since it was the generosity of Russians which had kept them alive till they were ransomed.

The Russian ambassador took the chain, smiling benignly at the sailors' thanks. I tried to explain what he was being thanked for. But I found the Russians already convinced that this, and all the other honours done to them, were a tribute to the terror inspired by their Tsar. At this they were triumphant.

But they were not happy. The next day I found them grumbling at their lodging, which was in the Monastery of San Domenico. The monks there look after every distinguished visitor to Venice. The guest-rooms were nobly furnished, and I did not at once understand the Russians' complaint. Father Possevino was not there to help me; he had gone to see the Doge.

There was no mistake; the Russians were saying they felt cold. How could men from Moscow be cold in Venice? It was not yet winter. A shivery wind was blowing across the lagoon, but the sun was warm. The Russians insisted that they had been cold at night. They fingered with disgust the thin Italian blankets. They pointed with disgust at a small charcoal brazier.

All our lodgings north of the Alps had been furnished with great stoves of brick or tile. I could not ask the monks to install such a stove during our three days at Venice. But I told the Russians that at Rome we should find Bohemians or Germans, who knew how to build stoves.

I had not yet convinced them of this when messengers came from the Doge, with presents – magnificent collars of solid gold. The Russians put the collars on, and then said that their own country made such things. What they really wanted were robes of heavy silk, like those the Doge and the Senators wore. I must go at once and explain this to the Doge.

I refused. Feeling the destiny of the Faith in Russia trembling within my hands, I nevertheless insisted that they must not insult the Doge. If they wanted silk robes I would take them along the Merceria, and they could buy what they liked. They were quite rich enough; in Vienna the Emperor had lavished gold upon them. This dispute became entangled with the dispute about the stove, and I was hard put to it to find the right words. Then more messengers came. These were Greeks who lived in Venice. They spoke Italian very badly, and seemed not to understand anything I said. In desperation I went running to the Rialto, to find a Greek interpreter.

What is there the Rialto cannot provide? I was very soon back with a Venetian who spoke (he said) seven languages. But the Russians and their visitors had disappeared. The monks of San Domenico told me that, the minute my back was turned, Greeks and Russians had perfectly understood one another. They had all gone out "like brothers".

Father Possevino came hurrying in. He exclaimed: "The Greek Church! Quick! We must be there first."

The Greeks had already taken the Russians away in a gondola — "a big one," the men at the landing-stage told us.

"Then we will take a small one," said Father Possevino, "and go by the side canals."

As we slipped along, scraping the green slime of back walls, narrowly dodging the rubbish thrown from back doors, Father Possevino explained that the Doge, after much other conversation, had remembered to mention the Greeks. They were permitted to have their own church in Venice, and the Doge had given them leave to invite the Russians to a service there. He said he saw no harm in that.

"No harm!" cried Father Possevino. "No harm, in the toleration of error!"

The rich merchants of the Greek colony were drawn up on either side of the entrance to their church. It was evident that their guests had not yet arrived, and indeed we soon saw them, alighting from their cumbrous gondola. Father Possevino stood in their way, and held up his crucifix.

The Greeks could speak Italian when they liked. "We have the Doge's permission," they said.

"But not," said Father Possevino, "the permission of the Tsar." He repeated this to the Russians, adding: "I must answer for you to your Tsar. I have his orders to conduct you to Rome, to show you the churches of the Catholics, not the churches of the Greeks! What shall I say, when I appear again before Ivan?"

That name was enough. The Russians had looked with

longing at the church. But the thought of their Tsar's anger parted them from the Greeks, and put them quietly into our gondola. I proposed a visit to the Merceria to buy silks, and they agreed without a murmur. While they and I were thus engaged, Father Possevino hurried back to see the Doge.

In the crowd passing up and down the Merceria, I once more began to lose the Russians – not all at once, this time, but by ones and twos. "They'll soon be back," said Molvaninov, smiling. And sure enough, within half-an-hour, they were. I was horrified when they admitted that they had been sampling the famous Venetian courtesans. But this was nothing to my horror when Molvaninov said, smiling more broadly than ever, that he preferred boys.

"Even that is a lesser sin than the toleration of heresy," said Father Possevino, when he returned from the Doge's Palace.

This time the Greeks had been ahead of him. He had found the whole Senate in session, listening with sympathy to the Greeks' complaint that they had been insulted. This insult, the Greeks were arguing, was directed against the Venetian Republic, since it was the Republic which tolerated their church.

In reply, Father Possevino warned the Senate that this toleration was a danger to the state. "It was useless to tell them the evils of heresy," he explained to me afterwards. "Half of them are Lutherans at heart, or atheists. I reminded them that the Greeks were subjects of the Turkish Empire, and probably spies. The Greeks made a great noise, clamouring that the Turks were their worst enemies. But the Doge spoke very courteously to me, saying Venice would always remember that I had ransomed its poor sailors. He was sorry that we were set on leaving tomorrow – meaning, of course, that he was not sorry! He knows that if I were to stay I should not rest until I had seen that Greek church exorcised, and made into a Catholic one."

We did not feel at ease until we reached Bologna, one of the Papal states. Here we found men who honoured Father Possevino, not only for his courage or his humanity to captives, which he regarded as means to a greater end, but for that end itself. What mattered (the Papal governor understood) was to bring heretics back to the Catholic Faith. It was to this end we were given a princely welcome. Amid the chanting of the monks, the cheering of the people, I heard the Russians telling one another that Bologna too must be afraid of Tsar Ivan.

In order to stay within the Pope's territory, we did not go by Florence, but through Rimini to Loreto. That holy place moved the Russians to tears; it was, they said, like one of their own places of pilgrimage. At last, one winter evening, we fell on our knees, seeing through the twilight the lights of Rome.

We stayed that night at Borghetto, and in the morning all the noblemen of Rome came riding out to meet us. As we entered the city we heard the salute from the cannons of the Castel Sant' Angelo. The Piazza del Popolo swarmed with the carriages of bishops and cardinals. Rome had indeed altered; there were no women in the carriages.

By the door of Santa Maria del Popolo stood a group of men in threadbare habits, the Jesuits. I felt proud that these men in black had done more than all the crimson cardinals to sustain the true glory of Rome. Among them, not marked out by any splendour but what God had planted in his face, was the General of our Society, Father Aquaviva. I gave him the Father Superior's letter, and received his blessing, which was more to me than all Rome.

The Russians were patient through High Mass in Santa Maria. They smiled afterwards, riding along the Corso, with the people cheering and shouting, and leaning out from every window to shower us with evergreens. At the Piazza Venezia we turned left, into the Colonna Palace, where the Russians were to stay. There was at last no need to lodge them in separate buildings; the Colonna Palace is so vast that the ambassador, with his favourites, could stay in the central building, and the other two factions in separate wings, hearing no more of one another than London hears of York. Such was Roman hospitality that, in every room where a Russian was to sleep, some German workman had installed a tiled stove.

The Pope, who had been ill, was recovering in Frascati.

While we waited for his return we showed the Russians the city. They still tried to tell us that their Tsar had palaces as big. But when they were shown that many of the Roman palaces were hospitals, orphanages and schools, they fell silent.

By narrow and poor streets, we came suddenly to St. Peter's. The Russians were astounded. Inside, they at last admitted that nothing in their country could equal this.

I showed them the statue of St. Peter, the toe polished smooth by the kisses of pilgrims. I myself kissed it, giving thanks that I had been permitted to see Rome again. But the Russians thought that only the face of a saint's image ought to be kissed, and the saints in St. Peter's are set too high.

Father Possevino told me to show them the English College. Here I was a poor guide; I could not restrain my tears at hearing my own language. The last words I had heard in English had been Edmund Campion's farewell. Now my countrymen showed me, set in a frame, on an embroidered cloth, a piece of the rope which had bound Edmund Campion to the hurdle. "Nobody could come near enough to dip a handkerchief in his blood. The sheriff's men kept them away."

The Russians questioned me. Were these fifty young men at the college all English, and yet Catholic? "The English in Moscow tell us that England has no respect for the Pope. They say that your Queen Elizabeth is head of her own church. Our Tsar admires her for that."

I explained that a great many English people clung to their ancient faith. To help them, these fifty Englishmen were studying, so that they could return to their country in secret, as priests.

"When Queen Elizabeth's men catch a priest," I went on, "they put him to the torture, to make him tell the names of his friends. When the priest refuses to speak he is put to death as a traitor — that is, dragged along the streets on a hurdle, hanged until he is half dead, then cut down, then gutted and castrated, his testicles and entrails being burned before his face, while he bleeds to death. And this was how my dear teacher, Edmund Campion, died."

But here my fellow-countrymen had news for me. The execution of Edmund Campion and his comrades had been supervised by a young nobleman. Though a Protestant, he had insisted on giving them a merciful death. They were hanged until they were quite dead, so that the last indignities were performed on lifeless bodies.

This news had been brought to Rome by Father Robert Parsons, Campion's friend, who had been with him on the English mission, and had escaped by the skin of his teeth. "He was here not six months ago," my fellow-countrymen told me. "What a pity you missed him! He was telling us what good company Campion was — how they joked and laughed together about their escapes."

I looked again at the relic — this poor piece of rope. What could it mean to the Russians?

But the Russians had what they call *chootkost* — a feeling for others' feelings. Because I kissed the relic, they kissed it as well, with reverence. Because I was weeping they wept, embracing me in furred and bearlike arms.

The next day Molvaninov asked me: "These men Queen Elizabeth has put to death — were they trying to overthrow her?"

"Oh no!" I said. "All our priests who go to England are forbidden to meddle with politics. They are to tell the people that the Government, however bad, must be patiently endured."

"But, according to the English merchants in Moscow, these priests write secretly to a queen who is in prison, one Maria."

"The Queen of Scots? No, they don't write to her."

"But they think she ought to be their queen. And they hope that an army will come from Spain, and put her on the throne."

"Certainly not! Our priests have nothing to do with any foreign invasion."

"They say that a few years ago the Pope sent out a decree — what is it called here?"

"A Bull."

"And in this Bull he said that Queen Elizabeth's people must rebel against her."

"No, that wasn't what he said.That is . . . When Father Campion and Father Parsons went to England, the Pope made it clear that English Catholics were to obey the Queen, in everything but religion."

"The Tsar was amazed when he heard of this Bull. He swore he would never allow the Pope a foothold in Russia, to stir up his people against him."

"But that isn't what the Pope does."

"The Tsar has trouble enough with his own bishops — always begging him to reprieve rebels and traitors. He says they have no notion how to govern a state."

"The Pope knows how to govern a state," I said. "Besides being the spiritual head and father of all Catholics, he's the earthly ruler of Rome and the country round — in fact of all the places we passed through, after we left the Venetian republic."

"Then the Pope is a Tsar as well. Does he have traitors executed?"

"Yes, of course."

"You have not shown us that," said Molvaninov. "We would like to see that."

The execution I found for them was in the Campo de' Fiori. "A traitor?" said Molvaninov eagerly, as the man was led to the stake.

"In a way," I said. "A blasphemer, who denies Christ."

"Do you have to bring such people to trial? In Russia there's no need. When a man raises his voice against Christ or the saints, the common people instantly tear him to pieces."

The Russians looked with interest at the priests who walked behind the condemned man. "They are praying God to bring him to a better mind," I said, and added with pride: "Two of them are Jesuits."

"And those men beside him, talking to him?" asked Molvaninov. "Are they priests?"

"No, those are the Comforters — devout laymen who sit up all night with the condemned man, begging him to return to the Faith. You see that even now, at this last moment, they are holding out a picture of the Virgin for him to kiss."

24

"If he does kiss it, will he be reprieved?"

"No, but he would make a good end, and the people would pray for him."

Some of them, I saw with dismay, seemed to be praying for him already. I hoped the Russians would not see that. It startled me to find how many heretics there were in Rome.

The condemned man was refusing to kiss the picture, jerking his bitter, black-a-vised face away.

"What stubborn wickedness!" Molvaninov said. "It would bring misfortune on Rome, if he were allowed to live."

As the fire licked up his legs, I heard the heretic calling out to Christ — that invisible Christ whose presence, he doubtless believed, made all holy pictures a profanation. Molvaninov said with approval: "Yes, I see that your Pope is a real Tsar."

Soon there was no more to see and everyone dispersed, the Comforters going to a tavern for their traditional breakfast of sweet biscuits and Greek wine.

When we returned Father Possevino looked with concern at my face. "How white you are, Paul! Perhaps we should have found some other form of justice to show the Russians."

"They enjoyed it," I said. "It's only that ... you see, Father, in Bohemia, we used to tell the peasants that we did not mean to bring back the stake for heresy."

Father Possevino smiled. "There are a number of countries where we have to say that. Your own among them. Your countryman, Father Parsons, has written a pamphlet to that effect."

Briskly, he turned to the important business of the day. The Pope was back from Frascati. He would soon be receiving the Russians in audience, and we must prepare them.

The Russians expressed great horror at the thought of kissing the Pope's toe.

"It is always well washed," I said.

Father Possevino explained: "You are not doing this honour to a mortal man. What you actually kiss is the cross on the foot of his Holiness."

This too disgusted them. How could a man wear a crucifix

on such a base part of his body? And what sort of a man was this Pope? That nobleman we had seen in Venice – the one whose name meant "good companion" – wasn't he the Pope's bastard son? (They had heard this from the Greeks.)

I could see Father Possevino's temper wearing thin. So I hastily promised that, once the Russians had kissed the Pope's foot, he would give them splendid silk robes as presents.

"What colours?" Molvaninov asked.

Afterwards I told Father Possevino of my penitence for telling a lie.

"It is not a lie," he said, "if we do something to make it true." And he sent me to negotiate with the Pope's chamberlains.

I could not find the one who generally dealt with us. In one of the Vatican's endless ante-chambers I tried to explain the matter to an underling, who could not grasp anything, even my name. I had to repeat it several times, and spell it out, and so it caught the ear of an elderly man who was passing. He exclaimed in English: "Calverley! Isn't that a Yorkshire name?"

"Yes, but our branch of the family doesn't live in the village of Calverley. My father's house is near York."

"Oh, I've been to York. It never stopped raining."

"The sun shone there for me, when I was young."

"And how long have you been abroad?"

"Since I was fourteen. My parents sent me to Rome to be educated."

"As a priest?"

"As a Catholic. Becoming a Jesuit was my own decision. Because I met Edmund Campion . . ."

"Ah! You were one of Edmund's little angels."

I did not like his light way of talking about angels – much less, about Father Campion. But I could not rebuke him; he made me feel very young. So I simply said: "I went to Prague so that I could attend Edmund Campion's lectures."

"And do you know Robert Parsons?"

"Only by repute."

"Pity! Edmund's name counts for nothing here. Oh, a blessed martyr and so forth — but you see, he's dead. Whereas Robert Parsons is very much alive. If you'd had a letter from him, it would have opened all doors. However, I'm not entirely without influence myself. Did you say that your Russians wanted silk robes? I dare say that can be arranged. Like everything else here, it's a matter of how much money. . ."

This gentleman, Sir Francis Englefield, did indeed have influence. The next day, as the Russians walked stiffly and slowly towards the Papal throne, cascades of many-coloured silks and velvets were shaken out before their eyes. Molvaninov blinked, hurried forward, and kissed the Pope's toe. His companions did the same.

His Holiness Gregory the Thirteenth, a splendidly upright old man, thanked them graciously for the jewels and furs they had brought him. He expressed his "singular love" towards the Tsar, and added that he prayed for him constantly. All, in fact, went well, and the Russians passed the rest of the day in trying on their new clothes.

The serious conversations came afterwards. In carefully chosen parts of the Vatican (we had to keep the Russians away from the Sistine Chapel, because of the naked figures) the Pope's chamberlains made it clear that Ivan would get no soldiers, unless he embraced our Faith. Let him at least allow Father Possevino to establish one House of Jesuit Fathers in Moscow! The Russians thought this might be possible, but they must first go back to consult their Tsar. The Pope took the hint and gave them ample money for their journey.

By the beginning of March, 1584, we were ready to set out. Father Possevino and I had mastered the Russian language, as far as these noblemen knew how to teach it to us. One of their attendants was considered very learned; he could read. He taught me their alphabet, which Father Possevino already knew. We were trying to prepare a simple handbook of instruction in the Faith. At first the Russian who could read helped us to write, but when he understood our purpose he refused to tell us whether or not our grammar was correct. I used to test it in conversation, introducing some tricky sentence into my talk, making it sound quite unconnected with religion, and then asking: "How would you say that?" Father Possevino, the man who had remained impassive before Ivan, could scarcely keep from laughing. Afterwards he would praise my ingenuity. He began, even, to confide in me.

"Once they let us have this Professed House in Moscow, we can establish a hospital there, and a school. These will be great novelties to them. By and by they will see that new things can be good things, and this will make them ready to receive a religion which to them is new. The Tsar has a son, Dmitri, who is a baby; by the time we return he will be almost old enough to learn to read, and if we were his first teachers . . . Unfortunately this Dmitri is not the heir to the throne. But who knows what God may send? The thing is to work slowly. When they ask us if we have come to convert them all, we must be, as it were, a little economical with truth . . ."

I could scarcely believe that I was being treated as an equal by this great man, the bravest and wisest I had known, and to me the kindest. Walking beside him through the Vatican, I felt myself already in those forests to which we were to bring light.

Two days before the beginning of the journey, I was called before the General of our Society, Father Aquaviva. He said: "You are not to go to Russia. You are to be a student at the English College. Your superior will be Father Agazzari, who is the Rector there."

Neither questioning nor thanking, I bowed obedience. But my eyes were full of tears.

A few months before, they would have been tears of joy. To enter the English College was to prepare for going to England. My dear country—all the more dear, if it brought me martyrdom . . . But in my mind I was already converting Russia.

When I told Father Possevino, I wept without restraint. And yet he did not say one word of sympathy. He seemed utterly cold to me. I burst out: "Did you tell Father Aquaviva that I was not good enough to go with you?"

He turned his face away. In a hard voice he said: "You really should know better than to ask absurd questions. When you entered the Society you made a vow of obedience."

"Yes, Father. But I thought . . . I thought that after I had spent so many months in preparing myself for the Russian mission, my superiors could not, without some very strong reason — "

"Could not? Who are you to say that?"

"I meant I thought they would not wish to . . . Father! Don't be offended with me!"

I knelt at his feet, but still he would not look at me. I pleaded: "Father, let us at least part friends. I know it is your duty to tell Father Aquaviva the whole truth about me. I have no right to question that. I accept it; I have been found wanting . . ."

He cried out: "Oh, stop, stop!" and covered his face with his hands. I understood at last that he was weeping too.

When he had mastered himself he said quietly: "Paul, there is not going to be a Russian mission. I am to conduct the Russians as far as their frontier, and then take charge of the work in Poland. There is plenty to do there."

"But in Russia — "

"Must I remind you again of our vow of obedience? I took it as well as you. And I did not take it as if it were a child's game."

"Father, I know that our superiors need not give us reasons . . ."

"But in fact they have done so. Father Aquaviva and the Pope have told me that, considering the stubborn disposition of the Russians, the savagery of their Tsar, their habit of breaking every promise they make to a foreigner, we should be casting good men away to no purpose."

"But our preparations . . ."

"You must make new preparations, and go wherever Father Parsons may send you. He is a real example for you, Paul. His heroic mission with Campion . . ."

"I know it will be an honour to obey Father Parsons. And yet – these months of work, all wasted!"

"If you think that God allows any work, done to His glory, ever to be wasted, you are not fit to be a Jesuit. Father Oviedo laboured years in Ethiopia, without result – that is, without result the eye of man can see. Do you think that in the eye of God his work was wasted? And then Sweden . . . the work I did in Sweden . . . just because it's all undone, all, all to do again . . ."

I said: "But Father, you *did* convert the King of Sweden."

"He has relapsed. He relapsed on the death of his Catholic wife. His conversion was always, you might say, conditional. If the Church would allow Swedish Catholics to hear Mass in their own language, read the Bible in their own language . . . His Holiness took the view that this was impossible. You see, His Holiness and Father Aquaviva have reports from the whole world. They know what our Jesuit missionaries are doing in India, in Japan . . . And they know how apt we are, in our ardour to convert the pagans to Christianity, to bend Christianity towards paganism. It's a failing I have been deeply guilty of. I am not fit to undertake the conversion of Russia. God willing, it will be done, but by more worthy hands than mine."

The Russians had tried my patience a dozen times a day, quarrelling, drinking, hiding shameless women and boys in the corners of the Colonna Palace. When it came to parting, they stroked my beard, and made me purr, and roared with laughter. Then they and I dissolved in tears.

Father Possevino did not. We both knew that, as a Jesuit must have no father and mother, he must have no particular friends. But I told him: "I shall think of you in England. When I am in danger, or in prison, or called upon to solve some entangled case of conscience, I shall think: *What would Father Possevino do?*"

"You must not ask that," he said. "The question is – what does God want me to do?"

III

AT THE ENGLISH COLLEGE, which I entered the same day,
I was taught many ways of asking that question. God wants
us (for example) never to tell a lie. But must we be as truthful
as one former pupil of the College, who was arrested as he
landed in England? They asked him whether he was a
priest. He said he was — and thereby at once became liable,
under the new law, to execution as a traitor. True, by such
a public martyrdom he might bring some spectators back to
the Church. But would he not have won more souls by
going about and preaching, for as long as possible before
he was captured? Would God not have preferred him to lie?
Surely such a small evil is justified for the sake of a great
good?

Once he had us all placidly nodding agreement to this, our
lecturer, Father Garnett, snapped out: "Then you all believe,
do you, that the end will justify the means? You" — he pointed
to me — "tell the class how much evil God permits you to do,
for the sake of how much good."

I made poor work of this, and my companions did worse.

Father Garnett then showed us that we had not yet begun to think about the question.

Though most of my fellow-students were not Jesuits, all our lecturers were. The flashing dialectic, the clarity, the plotting of each move as part of a world-wide plan, which had first attracted me to the Society of Jesus, now ruled our curriculum. Nothing was left to chance; each case of conscience which we might meet in our native country was examined. Though we should be working far apart, with no chance of consulting together, a priest in London would impose the same penance for the same sin as a priest in Wales. Of course, in a sense, no two sins are ever quite the same. Exploring the shades of difference, Father Garnett wrote out possible cases, and gave one to each of us to solve. (He had very odd handwriting; I knew it at once when I saw it, many years afterwards.) We would write essays on these cases, and then discuss them in class.

For example . . . A priest cannot absolve a man who intends to commit a murder, but can he absolve one who is going to fight a duel? Suppose the man's honour has been so be-smirched that he cannot live among his companions unless he washes the insult out in blood?

"You still have to refuse absolution," Father Garnet said. "Because, of course, England is ruled by law. A man who wants to clear his name can do it through the courts. The argument of 'insulted honour' does not carry the same weight as it does here in Italy."

"Then would our duty be different," one student asked, "if we were hearing confessions in Italy?"

"Certainly it would," said Father Garnett. "The priests here are often confronted with people who can get no redress by law. And not only in Italy. We all came here—have you forgotten?—through countries at war, with soldiers roaming to and fro, breaking into houses, insulting women; with every road full of robbers and murderers. It often happens here that a good Christian man has to kill to defend himself and his family. Whereas England has been at peace for a century. In

32

England a man can travel alone and feel safe. People even travel at night."

The student who had asked the question, Christopher Bagshaw, said: "But we were talking of men who kill to defend their honour, not their lives."

Bagshaw had a drawl in his voice, and an air of mature confidence. He was older than any of us—older, in fact, than Father Garnett—and he made us feel it.

"As I have already told you," Father Garnett said sharply "no killing for honour can be justified in England. Has anyone else a question?"

A quiet, serious young man, Robert Southwell, asked: "Can we give absolution to a man who intends to assassinate a tyrant?" Robert was going on to make the usual provisos— that the tyrant really was intolerable, that his heart was hardened against all remonstrance, that there was no hope of peaceful redress . . . Father Garnett cut him short.

"I did not think I was dealing with complete fools! Is anyone going to ask me a sensible question?"

After the lesson Christopher Bagshaw came up to Robert and me. He liked to tease us, and we could not tell him to go away, because it was the rule of the College that all private conversation must be in threes. Robert and I delighted in each other's company, but, when we had nobody to make a third, we had to part for solitary meditation. So we bore it as best we could when Christopher said to Robert: "Congratulations! You really succeeded in making him lose his temper."

"No," said Robert. "*You* did. Why do you always provoke him? I know you were a great man at Oxford once. But surely you can still find things to learn?"

"Too many things!" Christopher said. "Too much for my poor addled wits. I have worn them out in trying to get straight answers to straight questions. Do you know now if the Church will allow an Italian to fight a duel? Or if it's permissible to kill a tyrant?"

I said: "You didn't give him time to answer properly. As a rule they do give us answers."

"I grant we had a straight answer yesterday," Christopher said. "We asked if a Catholic might ever, in any circumstances, attend a Protestant service. The answer to that was no. But will you tell me this? If an Italian can kill a man in a duel, because that's the custom of the country, why can't an Englishman follow the custom of his country?"

"Because that's mortal sin," Robert said.

"Worse than killing a man?" drawled Christopher.

"In a way it is," I said. "A murderer knows he's done wrong; he may repent. But a heretic spreads the notion that wrong is right; he puts people in such confusion that they can't repent. That's why my mother and father stood out against going to the Queen's churches. Their neighbours were always telling them — it's a matter of form. You can come straight back from the Protestant service and hear Mass in your own house. We all do it, they said. We're all Catholics at heart. My mother used to say — how can you be a Catholic at heart, if you're not one in practice? And what's the use of keeping a priest in your house, an old man from Queen Mary's time, if there's not going to be a young priest to take his place when he dies? And what about your children? Are they to grow up thinking that the Queen's churches are the Church? Now you can see my mother was right. Because these weak-kneed Catholics, who've been going to Protestant churches for more than twenty-five years, have made England look to the world like a Protestant country. Another twenty-five years — another generation — and it really will *be* a Protestant country."

"But you and I," said Christopher, "are going to prevent that."

"With God's help."

"Well! I only hope we live long enough."

"Why shouldn't we?"

"On this food?"

By now Robert and I disliked Christopher Bagshaw so much that we would not join him even in grumbling at the food. But we could not bring ourselves to say that it was either good or sufficient.

"Lost your tongues?" Christopher asked. "Perhaps you want to die of consumption? Someone does, in this place, every six months or so. If they paid as much attention to our bodies as our souls . . ."

"The soul must always come first," Robert said. He alone could say such things without being mocked; he said them so earnestly and sweetly. In my first four months at the College, from the middle of March until the middle of July, 1584, I spent every hour I could with him. Though he was my fellow-student, and the same age as myself, he was allowed to lecture in one subject — our English language. Some of the students had come abroad as young children; they spoke English with an Italian accent, and were often at a loss for a word. Since I had lived in my own country until I was fourteen, I thought my English perfect. But Robert laughed at my new-fangled words, constructed out of Greek or Latin — "holocaust", for example, or "contamination". He said that the word "victim" was French, not English. I cast my mind back to my child-hood. Surely my parents and their friends were victims of persecution? What had they called themselves, if not that? "Sufferers" Robert suggested. I in my turn laughed at him for calling our kitchen servants "droils" — a good word for drudges who toil, but who else ever used it? And both of us had new words to learn from the most recent arrivals. We heard, for example, of people called "Puritans" — a small sect of Protest-ants who wanted Queen Elizabeth's church to be still more fierce against Catholics.

To regain his fluency, Robert used to write poems in English, and he made us all do the same. My own poems were poor stuff; I contented myself with setting Robert's to music. Indeed, the words danced, before ever I gave them a tune.

> Shun delays, they breed remorse;
> Take thy time, while time doth serve thee,
> Creeping snails have weakest force;
> Fly their fault lest thou repent thee . . .

35

I taught my companions the old holy songs of England—
"The holly and the ivy", "I sing of a maid", and many more.
With every note we sang England seemed nearer. When we
heard the bells of Rome toll for the death of Pope Gregory the
Thirteenth, and a fortnight later ring out for the election of
Pope Sixtus the Fifth, we thought of these events as far away,
although in fact they happened just across the Tiber.

The Rector of the College, Father Agazzari, heard our
singing and was delighted. He arranged that every Sunday
morning, after Mass, we should sing for a while in the fashion
of our country. Though to us they appeared somewhat rustic,
the old songs caused what the Italians call a *furore*. The
nobility of Rome came every week to hear them, putting silver,
and even gold, into our alms-boxes.

Our studies now included French, because we were un-
likely to reach our own country without passing through
France. Though I had come that way when I was fourteen, I
had almost forgotten the language. I learned it as I had learned
other languages, by putting the words to music and singing
them.

Our bodily exercises were directed to one purpose—to
prepare us for imprisonment. It was our duty to escape if we
could. Father Garnett brought in a sailor to teach us the art of
climbing down ropes.

"All the best prisons are provided with ropes," murmured
Christopher.

Father Garnett took us for a short walk, and showed us the
walls of the Castel Sant'Angelo. "There!" he said to Christopher. "Benvenuto Cellini escaped from that, by knotting the
sheets of his bed into a rope. What a scoundrel can do to save
his own skin, you surely do to keep the Faith alive in England."
Afterwards he made the sailor show us how to tie secure knots.

Father Parsons wrote from Rouen about the latest English
methods of making priests denounce those who had helped
and sheltered them. Father Garnett made us prepare for this
too. Just as every Jesuit, in his novitiate, does the Spiritual
Exercises, pacing his way step by step through Heaven,

Purgatory and Hell, so we went step by step through an English dungeon. In the baking heat of Rome in July, we closed the double shutters on our windows, and imagined a cold place, with water running down the walls, and a stench rising out of the floor. We had heavy fetters fastened on wrists and ankles, and made believe they froze our flesh. We did this for one whole day, eating nothing, and drinking only water, and by nightfall we were shivering with real cold. When at last we stumbled into the courtyard, we did not feel its heat.

The next day, still fasting, we were made to stand facing the wall, motionless, with our palms flat on the wall above our heads. This does not sound like torture, but the weariness, the aching in every part, the fits of cramp, grow past bearing within half an hour. Still we were not allowed to move, while Father Garnett pestered us with questions. "Your name? Your father's name? Where were you born? Where were you taught? What was your teacher's name?" Anyone who gave him an answer had a black mark. There was a black mark, too, for the first who sank to the floor.

On the third day of the fast, each of us had to go into a darkened room alone, and lie down on a wooden bench, and imagine it was the rack. I lay repeating the prayer I had learned by heart. "Oh Lord God, Thou wilt not permit me to be tempted beyond my strength. The worst these men can do is kill me, and I have often wanted to give my life for Thee. Thou canst do all things, Lord, and I am in Thy keeping."

How often I said this I do not know. I had lost all sense of time. My hunger, which had bitten my guts on the first day, and had been a dull continual pain on the second, was gone. Only I felt very light, as if I were floating.

Perhaps, I thought, I was about to have a vision. I had never had one, however I prayed or fasted. Our Founder, Ignatius Loyola, had actually seen the consecrated bread and wine change into the body and blood of Christ. I did not aim so high; only I hoped that one day I might see some bright creature walk across a meadow towards me, and watch the majesty of her arched brows, and the cheeks' glowing, and then observe (and, observing, fall on my knees) that the flowers did not bend beneath her tread.

Instead of a vision, I heard some real screams. I forced my tongue to continue its prayers, while my mind floated away. What sort of men were they, who earned a living by torturing other men? Could they have English faces? English voices?

Four men came in, whose faces I could not see, whose voices I did not know. They tugged at my arms and legs, and one of them asked me how much pain I thought I could endure. He spoke English with a strong Italian accent, and the fancy which crossed my mind was: "They cannot find Englishmen to do this work. They have hired bandits."

I told the men they were dislocating my joints. They laughed, and pulled harder. They pulled each finger slowly and separately, asking me for the names of my father, my mother, my superiors. They bent my fingers backwards. The Italian voice cried out: "Go on, confess! Your companions have all confessed. They've denounced you."

"Your own mother's turned against you," said another voice. Surely that one was English? And this one: "Were you carrying letters? What was in them?"

All these voices began to shout together, but I did not hear what they said. I was listening to a new voice, that whispered into my ear: "You didn't know what was in that letter, did you? You've been fooled by the man who sent you."

By now I had no doubt that this was real. It was Rome, the College, the safety, the singing, which were dreams of the past. I was in London, in the Tower. Couldn't I feel them tearing me limb from limb? I heard another voice—my own— shrieking: "Kill me, then, kill me! I shall never tell you anything!"

I came to in the courtyard. Father Garnett was clucking over me, fanning me, sponging my brow.

"You faint easily," he said. "That's good."

"Easily!" I cried out. "You don't know what they did, those hired bandits."

"He's wandering," someone said. Without turning to see the

face—I could not move my shoulders—I knew by the Italian accent that this was Father Agazzari.

"What hired bandits?" asked Father Garnett. "What do you mean?"

I said: "Why, those four men who were tormenting me. They've broken my bones; I can't move. They mustn't do it to the others! Tell them that! Please tell them; they can't be far away."

Father Garnett and Father Agazzari, and two other lecturers whom I had not noticed before, all burst out laughing. They said: "Did you really not know us?"

They helped me to my feet. Not only could I move; I could walk. The pains I had thought so intense were not there.

"A lad with vivid fancies," remarked Father Agazzari.

Father Garnett said: "But the fainting is good."

Father Agazzari agreed. "He can't talk while he's unconscious. But he was unconscious—what?—two minutes? Three? They could simply take him off the rack, bring him round, and then torture him again."

I staggered before the onset of another faint. This time I came round in my own bed, where I was ordered to stay for the rest of the day. A lay brother from the kitchen brought me some broth. I could scarcely swallow it, for tears. I had disgraced myself. I would never be sent to England.

I thought of one possible consolation. Since I was a coward and a milksop, my superiors might let me go to Russia after all. It was reasonable that they would not risk so fine a man as Father Possevino. But nobody would mind losing me.

The lay brother came to take my plate away. I had, after all, succeeded in eating the broth.

"Here's a letter for you," the lay brother said.

It was from Father Possevino.

"To Paul, my dear son . . . By God's grace, I have brought the Russians back to their country, feeling the want of your help every day. When we drew near the frontier, we heard the Tsar was dead. God struck him in the very act (so they say) of trying to dishonour his daughter-in-law. This lady's

39

miraculous escape has made the people consider her a saint. Her husband, the new tsar, is a simpleton. Her brother, one Godunov, is the real ruler, and he is hand in glove with the English heretics. By their influence an edict has been issued, forbidding any Jesuit to set foot on Russian soil. So our General's decision was almost a prophecy."

There was then some praise of myself, which, as things were, made my tears flow faster. Yet I read the letter over and over, so intently that I did not see Father Agazzari standing by my bed.

When he spoke to me I tried to scramble to my feet. He made me lie down again.

"Rest!" he said. "Rest! You are still very weak . . . May I read the letter?"

He had, of course, no need to ask. It was his right, as Rector of the College, to see everything we received.

As he read he remarked: "So the English will be ruling Russia now!" I felt my familiar temptation, my pang of pride. But this was at once extinguished when I saw how he smiled — in mockery, surely — at the praises of myself. "Yes, Paul, this is just what he told us about you."

I burst out: "Reverend Father, I know very well I am not good enough to go to England — "

"What's this?" Father Agazzari said. "Why, Paul, don't you want to go?"

"Of course I want to, but — "

"Don't say 'of course', Paul. There is no 'of course' about martyrdom. How old are you?"

"Twenty-three."

"Then you must have been a child when you knew Edmund Campion."

"I was nearly nineteen when he said farewell to me in Prague."

"A child, a child! How wise our Founder was, to lay it down that we do not take final vows until we are thirty! You may still decide not to be a Jesuit."

"Do you mean, Reverend Father, that I am not fit to be one?"

"If I meant that I should say it. But why should I?"

"Because of my cowardice."

"What cowardice? You did not beg for mercy, or offer to tell us anything. When you screamed, it was in defiance. And yet at that moment you believed that you were on a real rack, with real torturers. You were so far gone you did not recognise my voice."

"I knew it was an Italian voice, but somehow . . . Who was the other one, the one who whispered in my ear?"

"Nobody whispered, Paul. We were all shouting at the tops of our voices."

"But . . . I thought somebody whispered. It was the voice of an Englishman. But a rough, common Englishman. There's nobody like that here. It said: 'You didn't know what was in that letter, did you? You've been fooled by the man who sent you.'"

"Paul, I said you had a vivid fancy. Don't look so downcast! That's praise."

"Praise?"

"Oh, yes. What is a soldier's drill, except a means of making him imagine danger? If he has never seen it in his fancy, he will run away when he sees it in fact. Your fancy has prepared you well for England. I'd ask Father Parsons to send you, if it were possible. But our General, Father Aquaviva . . . You know, I suppose, that his nephew has been martyred in India? Not that Father Aquaviva could be shaken in his purpose by any personal grief. He always has disliked the sending of young men to a fate which is absolutely certain. And we know now that the English minister Walsingham sees all our letters, deciphers all our codes. He seems aware of every thought in every head in Rome. Which priests we're sending to England he certainly knows. His men wait at the ports with names, descriptions . . . Paul, every Jesuit in England has been captured. Every single one."

"Then there's all the more need for us to take their places."

Father Agazzari shook his head. "Even Robert Parsons, with all his experience — his great skill in avoiding capture — even he has been forbidden to set foot in England again. Father Aquaviva has ordered us not to throw away lives. Which we have been guilty of, even here in Rome. You young people are so ardent, it is easy to forget that you need food and rest. All this consumption . . . You are not ill, are you, Paul?"

"No, Reverend Father; only weak from fasting."

"You will grow strong again — we all will — when we move to Tivoli. Father Aquaviva has ordered us to stay there, in the hills, until the hot weather is over. And afterwards, Paul, you will be ordained priest, if you are sure . . . if you are quite sure . . . No, don't weep! We shall find you plenty of work. It's only that we don't as yet know where."

IV

THIS NEW DISAPPOINTMENT I tried to face like a Jesuit. I found some comfort in comforting Robert Southwell. He longed for England as I did, and found it as easy as I did to fancy that he was there. It was his cries I had heard in our imagined racking. He, like myself, had believed he was really being tortured. Only he did not faint. He struggled until they let him go, and then still struggled, feeling imaginary bonds.

Most of the students had treated the whole thing as a tiresome piece of play-acting. Christopher Bagshaw had flatly refused to take part in it, and had been expelled from the College. It was his fate which caused most agony to Robert Southwell.

"But Christopher was quite willing to leave," I said. "He never would have made a priest. His mistake was coming to the College in the first place."

"Supposing we should be told that?" said Robert. "You and I? If our superior said we had made a mistake, that we were not after all fit to be Jesuits . . ."

"We always have to obey our superior."

"Oh yes, if he tells us not to go to Russia, not to go to England, to wait and wait . . . But if he tells us to leave the Society, then we can disobey."

"Who says so?"

"It stands to reason. If he excludes you from the Society of Jesus, he must at the same time release you from your vow of obedience. So at that moment you can begin to dispute his decision."

"But then he can turn you out."

"No, he'd have to listen. I've thought of arguments he'd have to listen to. You, I'd say, you leave the Society first. See what the world outside is like, see whether you find more happiness there than here. If you do, maybe I'll follow you."

"I don't see why the superior should listen to that."

"Ah, but then I'd remind him that religion is not for the perfect, but for the imperfect. If even here — I'd say — within the Society, which gives us the most perfect surroundings we know, if even here I've shown myself imperfect, what will I be like in the world outside? Can you reconcile it with your conscience — I'd ask — to pitch me into that morass of sin? Even if I'm a nuisance to the Society — I'd say — even if I'm a great burden to it, can't the Society take its example from Christ, and shoulder the burden of my sins?"

We were sitting under a tree, looking down into the gulf of the River Aniene, and enjoying the sweet coolness that floated up from its tumbling waters. The move to Tivoli had made us very idle. We seemed to do nothing all day long but stroll about — not in twos, of course, but in threes. The student who was with Robert and myself, one Richard Sherwood, said: "You Jesuits are too clever for me. I can't keep track . . ." He went to sleep. I wanted to go to sleep. Only Robert wanted to stay awake and argue. I told him drowsily: "Put it into a poem!"

I awoke to find him tearing up the poem. "How can I write, when that pagan temple is leering at me?" He pointed to the top of the opposite cliff.

I remarked that the Temple of Sybilla had been turned into a Christian church.

"It's not right for a church," Robert said. "It looks *female*."

Richard Sherwood woke up and agreed. "You never see a heathenish thing like that in England."

In the autumn, after our return to Rome, we were all three ordained as priests. We knew how our parents would have rejoiced to hear us say Mass for the first time. They were a thousand miles away, and we could no longer even write to them. An assassin had killed the Dutch heretic leader, William of Orange. The English heretics put it about that the Jesuits were to blame. They prepared laws making it a crime to write to a Jesuit. To receive one, to give him shelter or food, might be punished with death.

And yet Richard Sherwood vanished from our midst. We heard he had gone to Rouen, where the great Father Parsons chose mission priests for England. At this Robert and I felt what no Jesuit should feel at the decision of a superior. Richard Sherwood was only half-educated, and a secular priest, not a Jesuit. Later we heard that Father Parsons had also sent a Jesuit into England. His name was William Weston. None of us knew him. He had been educated at another college, in Spain.

William Weston's companion, a lay brother, was arrested soon after he landed. But Weston himself escaped. So there was one Jesuit at liberty in our country.

At the beginning of 1585, Queen Elizabeth ordered that twenty priests, who had been in various prisons, should be put aboard a ship and sent to France. On the voyage they were warned that they would be put to death if they returned to England. But for the present the Queen was content to show them "notable mercy".

Why these twenty priests in particular? There were at least as many others, who remained in English prisons. Father Agazzari forbade us to speculate. He said that Father Parsons had met the deported priests in France; he was investigating the matter fully, and would come to Rome to report.

So this famous man, who controlled the secret ways to England, who chose the men to send there, would soon be with us. The prospect gave a new impetus to our studies. But another summer came, another August of drowsing and disputing by the streams of Tivoli. It was not until a Sunday in November, 1585, that I saw a stranger at Mass in our church. He wore the black habit of a Jesuit. His head was thrust forward; his bright brown eyes roamed about, studying our wall paintings, our Italian congregation, and ourselves. A smile played about his jutting features; he looked like a man who found it hard to sit still. This could only be Father Parsons.

I whispered my discovery to the rest of the choir. We made up our minds to surpass ourselves; our guest was to hear all our songs. Ralph, a boy with golden curls, whose voice had not yet broken, seized this opportunity to show what he could do. He was new to the College, and (though I had heard him rehearse) the purity of his tone astonished even me. Our Italian hearers were enraptured. Father Parsons, twisting and turning in his place, watched the Italians more than he watched us, the choir.

That evening he preached to us on the text: "Behold, I send you forth as sheep in the midst of wolves; be ye therefore as wise as serpents, and harmless as doves."

He told us that the twenty priests deported by Elizabeth did not themselves know why they had been chosen and others left. Those who speculated on the matter (Father Parsons darted his eyes at each of us in turn), those who suggested that these men had earned their freedom by making some concession to the heretics, were playing the heretics' game. The English Government had done this thing on purpose to sow doubt and division among us. Besides, their cruelty to priests had given them a bad name among the Catholic powers of Europe. They were now pretending to be merciful. They were putting it about that they did not persecute for religion, only for treason. It was against cunning such as this that we had to contend. We might, in our own country, meet smiles and fair promises, feather beds where we had expected the rack . . . But we were never to forget that these men were the same who had seized like wolves upon "my dear friend and comrade, Edmund Campion, whose martyrdom is painted upon my soul more brightly than I see it painted on the walls of this church."

The following afternoon we were summoned, one by one, to Father Agazzari's room. From the first one the rest of us learned that Father Parsons was there, asking questions – aimless questions, it seemed. "Who my father is, where I was born, whether I ever sang in the choir – all the things that Father Agazzari knows already."

"Was Father Agazzari there?"

"Yes, but he didn't say anything. There's another Englishman there too, a layman. Father Parsons called him 'Sir Francis'. He didn't say much either."

Soon it was Robert Southwell's turn. He came out after a long time, looking white. Before I could ask him what had happened, I myself was called in. I recognised the layman, Sir Francis Englefield, and thanked him for the help he had given me in arranging the visit of the Russians to the Pope. I bowed, as well, to the silent Father Agazzari. But my deepest reverence was for Father Parsons. I felt honoured that he should ask me questions.

"Your parents are good Catholics?"

"Yes, Father."

"You would not do anything to disgrace them?"

"I hope not, Father. I pray to be saved from any such temptation."

"Your singing in the church here – don't you find that this exposes you to temptation?"

"Yes, Father. When the nobility comes to hear us, when I see on one side of the church the ladies in their rich dresses, and on the other side the gentlemen staring at them, then sometimes I do feel a sinful inclination . . ."

"To lust?"

"Oh no, Father! To pride. I feel proud that our famous English music has drawn so many rich and worldly people. And then I consider how much the minds of these people are occupied with clothes, and the curling of hair, and the trimming of beards. And that makes me determined to sing so well that, by God's grace, a thought of His glory will penetrate even the thickest head. When it comes to my solo part, and I see that at the rising of my voice the rustling stops, and the whispering, that eyes no longer turn to gaze in other eyes, but are all fixed on the cross of Christ—then I feel such pride! And I am never sure how far it's a sinful pride in myself, and how far a just pride in the power of God's word over men."

"Are you sure that all those people are looking at the cross? Not at you?"

I was too much taken aback to reply. Sir Francis laughed and said: "Some Italian ladies think of a tall yellow-haired Englishman as a new toy."

Father Parsons went on: "I suppose you are never tempted by women?"

"I have been troubled with . . . certain thoughts, but by God's grace I have always been able to overcome them."

"Those Russians you escorted," said Father Parsons, "were much given, I believe, to sins of that kind."

"Yes, I'm afraid so."

"And to something still worse?"

"Their ambassador had horrible vices."

"You mean he was a sodomite? You think that horrible?"

"Of course."

"And yet," Father Parsons went on slowly, "you openly showed your affection towards the Russians."

"I tried to love them, Father, as Christ loved poor sinners, remembering that they were ignorant men, brought up in barbarism and heresy . . ."

"You think this vice of theirs happens only among heretics?"

"Oh! I hope so."

"And you a priest! Haven't you heard any confessions?"

"Not yet, Father."

"Nobody confessed to you what was going on under your nose in your own choir? You know a boy called Ralph?"

"What—the child?"

48

"About thirteen."

"Yes; he has a beautiful treble voice."

Father Agazzari spoke for the first time. "This morning we had to send him away. And two of the servants."

I cried out: "God have mercy on us!"

"I hope He may," said Father Parsons. "Did you really know nothing about this?"

"Nothing! I can hardly believe it yet. That little boy . . ."

"Oh, he was corrupted long ago," said Father Parsons. "He has lived among Dominican friars."

Father Agazzari turned to me, and then glanced back at Father Parsons. At last he succeeded in saying: "Paul, I have to ask you this. Do you think that your friendship with Robert Southwell is doing you any good?"

"Reverend Father! Nobody could know Robert without his doing them good."

"You love him?" asked Father Parsons.

"Yes."

The looks which ran between them showed me I was misunderstood. I cried out: "But not in a wrong way! I love him as a brother in Christ."

"And you think he feels the same kind of love for you?"

"I believe so. That is, I'm sure he does."

"Then it will surprise you," said Father Parsons, "to know that he has just admitted that your . . . beauty, he calls it, sometimes arouses his desire."

Father Agazzari jumped up and helped me into a chair, where I immediately fainted. As I came round I heard him saying to Father Parsons: "You see? Innocent, innocent!"

"Or simple-minded," Father Parsons replied. "The point is, this elaborate singing will have to stop."

I cried out: "Oh, no!"

"You are with us again, are you?" said Father Parsons. "Well! You've seen what your choir leads to. Don't you tell me that God needs polyphonic music to praise him. He can be worshipped very well in plainsong."

I still felt weak from the shock of what they had said about

Robert. I could not call them all three liars, but at least I could defend my music.

"Did the College do wrong," I asked Father Parsons, "when it employed a good artist to paint our martyrs? The Russians would think so. They said their modesty was outraged, when a painting in a church made women look like women, or men like men. But we are Catholics; we believe that what God wants of us is the very best we can do. The liveliest figures the artist can paint, the most cunning pattern of sound the musician can make —"

Parsons looked at me like a father sorrowing over a son. He said quietly: "So that's how it seems to you, Paul, is it?" After a pause he added: "Robert Southwell is not in the choir."

"No; he can't sing."

"You have him as one of your spectators. I watched you yesterday come forward like a player, to the exact spot where the sunlight caught your face."

"I stand where the resonance is best. The sunlight varies according to the season."

Father Parsons laughed shortly. "Innocent! Perhaps you don't share the feelings you arouse. Is a whore innocent when she feels nothing? But if, as you pretend, you don't care for your looks, you'll hide them under some dark dye, before you go to England."

"England!" I said. "If it's to go there, I'll dye myself till I'm black."

"That's not the way to avoid notice," remarked Sir Francis.

"But am I really to go to England?" I asked.

"Well, you can't stay here," said Father Parsons. "Even you can understand that. And you won't attempt to see your friend Southwell again."

I bowed, seeing that Father Agazzari had nodded. He was my superior; his nod was enough.

Father Parsons went on: "I suppose you'll make difficulties about starting for England this week."

"Today, if you like."

"Today's nearly over. You can't go travelling by night; you're not in England yet."

Sir Francis broke in suddenly: "Must you really send him to England?" (How dared he dispute an order? Of course, he was a layman.) Looking sidewise at Father Parsons, he went on: "What harm has this boy ever done you?"

"Sir Francis!" I exclaimed. "Going to England is an honour. It's what I've been preparing for, since I became a Jesuit — to save the souls of my fellow-countrymen."

Sir Francis laughed. "My dear boy, the English Catholics won't let their souls be saved. They won't countenance the only means of salvation — military help from Spain."

"If you mean an invasion," I said, "they are quite right. We could never spread the Faith by foreign soldiers, rioting round England as they do round Italy, breaking into houses, insulting women, forcing good Christians to kill in self-defence. Do we want to make England a country where people can't travel at night? That would be a strange way to spread the Faith."

"Good, good!" said Father Parsons. "You see, Sir Francis, this boy tells you what I have been trying to tell you for years. Our mission priests know they must never meddle in politics. No insults to Queen Elizabeth! No smuggling of messages to the Queen of Scots! Obedience to the Government in everything which does not directly concern the Faith!"

"Paul," said Father Agazzari gently, "I now appoint Father Parsons your superior."

So it was Father Parsons I must obey. In the words of our Founder, Ignatius Loyola: "I must let myself be led and moved as a lump of wax lets itself be kneaded, must order myself as a dead man without will or judgment . . ." That is, as a Jesuit. And yet I was not prepared for Father Parsons' first order.

"Go with Sir Francis Englefield. Do as he tells you. He will arrange your disguise."

Though Sir Francis had helped me at our first meeting, I had not much liked him then, and I liked him less now that I

51

had heard him talk treason. I thought, even, that he might be
an agent of Walsingham, trying to sound us out. Yet Father
Parsons, who had been so angry with him, not two minutes
before, was now trusting him with my safety.

Father Parsons, of course, must know best. English Catholics were always on the alert for spies; they must long since
have asked themselves whether Sir Francis was one, and
concluded that he was not. He must be an original, whose odd
views were tolerated by a few old friends . . .

I resolved not to take to heart anything he said. Yet I was
put out, when we reached his house, and he caught me
familiarly by the shoulder.

"Don't look so downcast, Paul! Or . . . Father Calverley, I
suppose I ought to call you, though you're young enough to be
my grandson. Robert Parsons gave you a rough time, I know.
He's fretting over the new Pope. The old one was all for the
Jesuits—gave that College of yours a big subsidy. The new
one stopped it dead. Parsons isn't used to finding doors locked
in his face. Besides, you hurt his feelings."

"I did? How?"

"Paul, my boy! A priest who's never heard a confession!
I suppose you can't make out what's wrong with Robert
Parsons."

"He is my superior," I said coldly.

"Ah! But he wasn't, when he began bullying you. He had no
right to give you orders then. Telling you what music you
were to sing, where you were to stand—what's that to him?
I'll tell you what it was to him! Parsons is the vainest man
alive. He can't endure to see another man look handsome."

I said: "But Father Parsons is dedicated . . ."

"Dedicated to the English mission. I know. When he went
to England in disguise, he was in his glory. Dressed as a
soldier, a feather in his hat, gold lace on his coat, such a pea-
cock, such a swaggerer . . . And what does he tell me to do
with you? Shave off your beard, dye your hair black, stain
your face gypsy colour—which is ridiculous! Your golden
hairs will come bristling out on your chin, every morning

before you shave. Against a dark skin they'd stand out like beacon lights! As for dyed hair—it always looks dyed. No; we'll have your beard off, but we'll leave you your natural colour."

I said: "But I have to obey Father Parsons. He's my superior."

"Not mine, though! I do as I think best. I've been putting you lads into disguise, long enough. Here—if you're to go clean-shaven, you'll need a glass every morning. I suppose in your college you don't use one?"

"No, never."

He gave me a small glass, backed with a Venus and Cupid in chased silver. It was a heathenish thing, but I took it so as not to offend him. He was pleased.

"There! That'll keep the innkeepers from thinking you're a priest. Now, will any of these doublets fit you?"

He opened a chest and brought out clothes of every colour, some very fine.

"I believe you'll be going as a merchant's clerk. We mustn't make you too grand. Try this on . . . Yes! You'll be a very pretty boy, when you leave Rome."

I could not understand why I should leave Rome in disguise. I had thought I could appear as a Jesuit, so long as I was travelling through good Catholic countries. But Sir Francis told me firmly: "Your disguise begins here! In this room! Don't you go without it one step of your journey, or you'll be caught like that fool Campion . . . You needn't glare like that, Paul. Saint he may have been, but fool he was for certain. He and Parsons went through Geneva. They had some reason—a Spanish army was marching through Savoy, and we all know we'd rather sleep among heretics than Spanish troops. Campion and Parsons carefully disguised themselves before they went into Geneva, and then they spoiled it all because they couldn't resist a good upper-and-a-downer with some Calvinists. They actually went to the chief man there, Beza, and asked him how he dared be a Protestant. Of course every word they said went straight to London. Parsons thought it wouldn't matter; he was so clever that he could always escape. Well! He did – by the skin of his teeth. Campion walked into a trap. They caught him at Dover, only the mayor was a secret Catholic, and let him go. He couldn't rest until he was caught again. That's the trouble with all you angels, Paul."

"I'm not an angel."

"You're innocent enough. Trusting Italians, because they seem to be Catholics! Why do you think I have to do all this myself? Why don't I bring a tailor in? For years we thought we were safe, if we disguised our boys in front of Italians. How could an Italian be a spy for Walsingham? We forgot how many of them had some secret grievance. Friends burned by the Inquisition – that sort of thing."

The clean-shaven, long-legged man, staring out of the mirror at me, did not look like a merchant's clerk. Yet I was to be one, I learned the next day. I was to travel with one Minello, a silversmith, who was hoping to interest the French court in the new Italian custom of eating with forks.

"He doesn't know you're a priest," Sir Francis explained. "He asked the Jesuits for a secretary, because they educate young men so well. I suppose you write Italian, Paul? And French? You're to travel as far as Paris with Minello, and then kiss him goodbye. Go to the Duke of Guise's house; his men will help you to reach Rouen." He then told me that the Jesuit Fathers in Rouen would provide me with English clothes.

"And I hope they do it right this time! Don't you let them dress you in a servant's coat, and an embroidered shirt peeping out from underneath. Or send you to walk across country in riding boots. These English Catholics! There isn't one of them I would have kept as a page, when I was on the Privy Council."

"Were you a privy councillor?"

"Has nobody told you that? Yes, I counted for something when England was England, in Queen Mary's time. Not that Queen Mary took much heed of my advice. Too gentle for her own good. If she'd followed the right course in time, with Elizabeth . . . Still! She didn't, so here we are. Elizabeth has just succeeded, you know, in seizing my estate. I thought she couldn't. I made it over to my nephew years ago, before I left England. But Elizabeth found servants to twist the law hard enough, in the end . . . God, Paul! How young you look, without your beard! A child! Is your mother alive?"

"She was two years ago. I haven't heard since."

"Better seek her out, then. A lad like you—you won't last long without a mother."

"You will not, of course, attempt to see your father and mother," said Father Parsons, when he came before dawn to give me my final instructions. "A Jesuit has no father and mother."

"Yes, Father."

"Your superior in England will be Father Weston—the only Jesuit still at liberty there."

"Yes, Father."

"You will find him by consulting Father Richard Sherwood (also called Carleton) in the tall house by the turnstile, in the north-east corner of Lincoln's Inn Fields in London. Oh, and while you are there, give Father Sherwood a letter from me."

Father Parsons gave me a wallet with a secret pocket, and in that pocket a letter. If I could not deliver it, I was to destroy it unread. "Not that you could read it," Parsons added. "It's in our new code—the one Walsingham doesn't know."

For fear of Walsingham's Italian spies, Father Parsons could not see me off, he explained. A link-boy was waiting to lead me to Signor Minello's house.

All this was whispered to me in a corner, while Sir Francis warmed his hands by a brazier, on the other side of the room. But when I kneeled for Father Parsons' blessing, Sir Francis came to kneel beside me.

The words he said then came back to me later, when I spent whole weeks of seasickness between Ostia and Marseilles. And again when I was riding through France, which was ravaged from end to end by the wars of religion. Tacking back and forth to avoid the armies, keeping out of woods to avoid the deserters, never setting foot on any road unless among a dozen other travellers, I remembered often what Sir Francis had said. I had company which was no company to me, for the silversmith Minello, almost illiterate, talked mainly about his money and his forks. When he tried to cheer me up, it was with stories which I did my best not to hear. Once especially, when we came to a town long famous for its inns, and found the whole place empty, the people massacred, the food all stolen, when we lay down supperless by the fire we had made in the ruins — then I remembered the strange words of Sir Francis. He must have known my journey would be like this. And yet he had said to Father Parsons: "I need a blessing too. I need it more, because my part is the hardest."

V

IT IS NOT EASY to clamber down a rope ladder, hanging over the side of a swaying ship. Especially if you are weak from seasickness, and so cold that your hands will scarcely grasp the rungs. The night was not pitch dark; I could see two men in the rowing boat below me. Soon I could hear them too; they were muttering at my clumsiness. Their words were foul, but their arms were strong; between them, they got me into the rowing boat.

I was not the only cargo. The French vessel which had brought me across the Channel now unloaded a variety of casks and barrels. Each one was let down by rope to within an inch of my head; and each one, as I ducked to avoid it, was caught in those hard arms which had caught me. Unhooking, untying, stowing away, the men in the rowing boat worked as fast as if it had been broad daylight. These were the first Englishmen — that is, Englishmen living in England — whom I had seen for almost eleven years.

As they rowed me away the French vessel shook out her sails, and was lost in the mist-watered moonlight. I looked round eagerly for land — English land. But I could see nothing; it must be a long way off.

It was now March, 1586, and I had done nothing yet. Perhaps I never should. Better men than myself had been arrested as their feet touched English ground. I ought to begin my mission at once, with these men; the souls of smugglers are certainly in danger.

I said: "You're fishermen . . ." and was about to add, ". . . like the disciples of Christ."

But one harshly shushed me, and the other whispered: "A voice do carrry over the water, sir, worse than the cry of a bird."

So I held my tongue for a while. But it fretted me that I did not know where they were taking me — not even the county. I had sailed so far, since leaving France, that I did not think it could be Kent. And yet Kent would have been convenient; the French vessel was going on to take her lawful cargo to London. Pitching my voice as low as the boatmen did, I whispered: "When do we land?"

The man who had shushed me muttered: "Last time I do ever take live cargo. They barrels do lie silent where we do put 'em."

But the other one answered me courteously: "Toozey, sir." "Where?"

"Han't you never heard o' Boozey Toozey? You'll be not above a dozen miles from Colchester."

Essex, then . . . I saw land so suddenly that I almost cried out. It seemed within arm's length. The reason I had not seen it before was its flatness; it scarcely rose above the water. For the first time since leaving France, thirty-six hours before, I did not feel sick. The boat bobbed up and down as fast as ever, but now I could fasten my eyes on the sweet steadiness of the shore.

One rower clutched the other's arm. They stopped and listened. In the pinching cold I bit my hand to stop my teeth from chattering.

There were sounds, of course. A low sound, of waves

lapping on the shore. A high sound, of a seagull waking to some danger. Pitched between these two, and coming from inland, the hoot of an owl. There was also, somewhere, a voice. Far off—perhaps a mile off—a man was giving orders, as a captain might to his crew.

The two boatmen, with one accord, turned the boat hard in to the soft shore. They pulled me out of my seat and pitched me bodily on to the sand. As I lay there, one man—the more courteous one—leaped out of the boat, rolled me over, and pulled my coat open. But the other one angrily hauled him back. On the instant they had pushed off again, and were gone.

So I was on English earth—soft, sandy earth, which, as I began to rise, trickled away from under me. I got to my knees and thanked God I had come so far. Then the cold forced me to rise and run.

But which way? We were always advised, when we landed at night, to hide in a wood until morning. But there were no woods here—only hillocks of sand, high enough to make my progress awkward, but not high enough to give me shelter, either against the wind or against the eyes of that captain I had overheard. I must get well inland before morning. Once it was light, I knew my part; the first carter or herdsman I met I was to encounter boldly, asking him if he had seen a falcon astray. The Jesuit Fathers in Rouen had carefully dressed me in the clothes of a falconer. The clothes were too new and clean, but no doubt a walk in rough country would put that right.

As I went inland I found the sandy hillocks higher, and firmer, being bound with grass. I stood on one and guessed, rather than saw, that smoother country lay ahead. There was a mist lying even as a carpet.

When I was down within the mist I was, of course, more lost than ever. I no longer felt the sea wind, so I could not find my direction by walking away from it. Nor could I keep to any direction long; the grassland was criss-crossed by ditches, some too wide to jump, some too deep to be forded, so that I had to follow the bank for a while, until I found a narrower place. I went back and forth, until I lost all direction. One ditch was like another; I had nothing to steer by, right or left, behind me or before. I looked up and found the moon, just visible through the mist. That would have helped me, if I had remembered where the moon had been when I started.

At last I found a path, a little wandering one, as might be made by a dairymaid's feet when she came to call in the cattle. Soon it broadened into a wide muddy track, marked by the feet of the cattle themselves. Was I near a farmhouse?

I stopped. Whether I could see it (as I fancied) through the mist, whether I could smell cowsheds and piggeries, whether I was aware of that lonely, foolish feeling, which comes to a man awake when he is near others asleep, I knew the farmhouse was there.

Farmhouses have dogs. I must go by another way.

By jumping another ditch, and crawling under a hedge, and crossing a ploughed field, I found a way. Indeed, I found a good broad cart-track, which must surely lead away from the farm, inland. I was out of the dead flatness now; the mist grew thinner, and I stepped out boldly.

I followed the track still, when it went down a slope, and into more mist. I did not see in time that I was coming to a tall building. It looked like a water mill. But there was no dog — or it would have barked already — and it was far too early for the miller to be up. I passed the mill as quietly as I could, and made for what seemed to be a bridge over a misty river.

A lantern swung into my face. "God!" said a voice. "Another priest!"

I said nothing. The voice went on: "You'd best come inside."

A hand guided me into the mill. I obeyed, not knowing whether this was hiding-place or prison.

The darkness inside was broken by a faint glow from a fire. "Sit down, then," said the voice, which did not sound either kind or unkind, only very weary. "I'll mend the fire."

As he poked it and threw in sticks, the fire lit this man's face. It was deeply lined, not yet old, but graven into a settled sadness.

"Will that do to warm you?" he said.

I spoke my first words to him. "Yes, thank you."

"Have to do for light as well. I need the lantern with me, when I open t'other sluice."

He picked up the lantern and went out, to resume whatever work my coming had interrupted. He did not lock the door. I might have run away.

Ought I to run away? This man had known at once I was a priest. Yet he had not knelt down to ask my blessing. Therefore, he was not a Catholic. And why should anybody but a Catholic risk his life to give me shelter? His only safety would be to betray me. Yet something made me feel he did not mean to do it. Perplexed, I began to pray.

The prayers were struck out of my mouth by a sudden thunderous noise. It shook the very chair on which I sat. There was the rushing of water, and the groaning of wheels, and the grinding of millstones — familiar sounds; once the shock was over I knew them all well enough. The smell was familiar, too, and English. A floury, dusty smell is common to all mills, but abroad it has another savour; the grain is different. This mill held the very air of my childhood, when I used to watch the corn being ground on my father's estate. It caught my throat. It set me dreaming, so that I almost forgot to wonder: what kind of a miller is this, who grinds his corn in the dark?

On his return he held up the lantern, looked at my clothes, and said: "They didn't strip you, then?"

"Who?"

"Why, the two that brought you. Butter-mouth and Grumble. Didn't they so much as take your money?"

"No," I said.

He looked up. "Hoppers be going down empty, by the sound. Have to see to that." And he was gone again. I heard his feet climbing a stairway above my head. Hunched on the chair, I put my head on my knees, and, amid the grinding and the shaking, fell asleep.

The miller woke me to offer me some of his breakfast —

bread, butter, cheese and ale. As we ate I asked him: "What makes you think I'm a priest?"

He said: "It's in your face."

"You mean anybody can see it?"

"I don't know what other folks can see. I keep my own eyes open. If they two think I don't know what cargo they carry . . . How can I help seeing, when they come at high tide, just as I have to get up to see to the mill?"

"Does your mill work by the tide, then?"

"Ay. Where'd you come from, that you han't seen a tide-mill?"

"I was born in Yorkshire. Our mills work by the wind, or by streams."

"Ah! Maybe there's hills, and the streams come down with a bit of a push. Do the millers there work in the daytime, and sleep at night, like farmers?"

"Yes."

"Lucky devils! Day or night, sick or well, I have to turn out when the tide sues –"

"When the tide *what*?"

"When it's on the turn, then. At high water, when the mill-pond's full, I go out and shut the sluice gate, to keep the water in. That's when I see . . . well, all I see, if you talk of seeing, is a stir in the bushes, a little way down the creek. Another man might miss it. But I know it's those two. Lunatic broth is what they land mostly – French wine. But this is the second time they've landed a man. T'other one asked me for a rag to keep him warm. They'd left him nothing but his shirt, and even that they tore. Knowing, you see, that he daresn't lay information against 'em. I told 'em, when they come here afterwards, trying to sell me some of their stinking foreign stuff, I told 'em – you've gone greedy. Rotten greedy. Next thing – I told 'em – you'll be taken."

"They nearly were, tonight. There was a voice on the water. They took fright and pitched me out on the sands."

"Then that's why they didn't rob you."

"I think one of them wanted to. The one with a more pleasant way of talking."

"Ay, Butter-mouth. He butters people up and robs 'em after. Old Grumble's more nasty with it. So they put you on the sands! Then you took a while, I reckon, finding your way. No wonder you didn't reach here until I was coming out to open t'other sluice."

"What other sluice?"

"Why, the one that works the mill. I have to wait until the tide's gone down a bit, so there's a difference in the level 'tween the millpond and the creek, and the water will fall heavy on the blades of the wheel."

"Then that's what you were doing when I came—opening the sluice."

"Ay."

"How long does the water run?"

"Two hours—not much more. Only a trickle a-trickling now—can't you hear?"

"Two hours! Did I sleep so long? It must be light outside."

"Ay."

"May I have some water for washing and shaving?"

"Pump's out there."

When I was ready to go I said: "You've been kind to me. Can I . . . That is, what do I owe you for board and lodging?"

"Sixpence'll do."

"There you are then—with my blessing."

"I'll take it without. Your sort never come here to bring us no blessings."

"We're . . . we're not what you've been told. Not traitors to our country. We only want to bring back the religion of our fathers."

"Ay. Bring th'old abbot back to Toozey."

"To where?"

"Toozey—the village there, over that bit of a rise. St. Osyth, it was called when the abbot was there."

"Do you really remember the abbot?"

"Ay. My dad used to take me up there, when he paid the

rent. The monks used to grab the money as fast as ever Lord Darcy do grab it now."

"Were you here when King Henry's men came, to turn the monks out of the Abbey?"

The miller laughed. "'Never!' th'old Abbot said. 'Pray for us,' he told the people. 'We'll all be holy martyrs.' King Henry's men came again, said: 'You go peaceably, you and your monks, there'll be a fat pension for everyone.' 'Ah!' said the Abbot. 'Ah! Oh! Pray for us, good people, we're going.'"

"Catholics aren't like that nowadays. We are willing to be martyrs."

"Ay. That's what I see in your face. Same as I see in my son's face. Daft young fool! Him and his religious notions! Why he couldn't bide in England —"

"What!" I said. "Has your son gone abroad to be a priest?"

"No, a soldier. He's in the Low Countries, wi' th'Earl of Leicester. It preyed on his mind, what the Spaniards were doing to the people. Have you been there, sir? Do you think those tales are true?"

I hesitated. Then I said: "There are cruel things done in any war."

"Ay, but when a town surrenders, when there's no more fighting, to turn the soldiers loose on women and children . . . My son said, if we didn't face the Papists there, we might have to face 'em here. Let 'em come, I say; we'll see about it then. But there's no reasoning with Nick. A rank Puritan! There's that look about the eyes . . . T'other priest who came this way, the one they robbed — he was an older man, past forty, and yet he had that look. I gave him Nick's old clothes. I thought — who knows if Nick's ever coming back to wear 'em?"

"Did he — the priest you gave the clothes to — did he get safe away?"

"Who knows? They never hanged him in Colchester; I'd have heard that. There's not many in these parts would give him away. We're not on speaking terms with justice. What with smugglers, what with Puritans . . . It's easier for the smugglers; they don't mind going to church."

"Don't the Puritans go to church, then?" I asked.

"Lord, no! Not a real Puritan wouldn't. They reckon the churches is too much like what they was in the Pope's days."

This was new to me. I had thought a Puritan was just a particularly noisy supporter of Elizabeth's church.

The miller was by now impatient with my questions. "Look, sir, that's your way, if you don't want to go through the village. Over this bridge, then follow that path. When you come to the cart-track, turn left. Keep your back to the breeze, and 'fore three hours are out you'll be at Colchester."

In a cold windy spring, with no leaves yet, in poor heath country — even then, how beautiful it is to be in England! The grey dawn melted into a lighter grey. I was never aware of a moment when the sun broke through, and yet softly I became aware of sunshine. The few people I passed, people driving their geese to the common, or gathering brushwood, first gaped at me, then smiled, then greeted me and the sun. "Good morning to 'ee, sir! And a beautiful morning 'tis, too!" Two young girls looked boldly into my face, then pretended to be shy, nudging one another and giggling. One was dark, one fair; but both had in their cheeks that soft English colour which I had forgotten. A woman with red hands was hanging out washing. "The Lord do know his own dear lambs!" she said. "It's a beautiful drying day!"

The cottages of these people seemed at first sight no more than bubbles in the mud. Looking more closely, I could see that the mud was plastered round a strong wooden framework, and surmounted by neat thatch. There were some signs of comfort — even glass in the windows. All the houses looked easy to burn, and this troubled me, because in France I had seen villages where every house that would burn was a blackened ruin. French faces had peered sidelong out of blackened rags.

Now I wanted to stop and gaze at each welcoming smile. I wanted to prolong each greeting into conversation about the love of God. These were my people. I melted with desire to do them good.

65

But I had first to reach London, see Richard Sherwood, and give him his letter. I could not remember how far Colchester was from London, but I thought it was farther than a man could walk in a day. Besides, the Fathers in Rouen had stuffed my wallet with money, telling me that I must ride, not walk. Inns were suspicious of travellers who came on foot. So I hoped that Colchester was a fair-sized town, where I might buy a horse.

That was what I told the watchman at the city gate. "I've come to buy a horse." He took this as reasonable, and pointed up the hill to the market place. The horses for sale were standing outside a church. Before I could reach them, some-one caught at my sleeve. My stomach turned as if I were at sea again. But this was not the law, merely a red-faced villain who wanted to sell me a brace of hounds. "Just the thing for a man who understands hunting." (My falconer's disguise, then, must be good.) I tried to walk past the red-faced man, but he was persistent. "Just look at them! Look at them!"

"I can see them," I said. "They're miserable, harried — more like the hunted than the hunter."

"Ah! But that's because they've only just been trained."

"Only just been whipped, by the look of them."

"Well, yes, my mate — he treats 'em a bit rough. Whips 'em, keeps 'em locked up without food a day or two. Then I come, let 'em out, give 'em a nice bit of meat. They'll do anything for me. Look how they lick my hand! Well, training dogs, you has to be a bit clever."

I escaped and found a horse dealer, another villain. I looked at the bony beasts he offered me, and said: "Haven't you anything better?"

"For your master, eh?" said the horse dealer, looking at my clothes.

To walk about the country dressed like a falconer was all very well. But on the beautiful chestnut gelding, which I managed to buy at last, I must look like a gentleman. At the Red Lion, where I had my midday meal, I asked: "Is there anyone here who makes good clothes?"

"I suppose you'll go to the Dutch," the innkeeper said sadly. "To me, sir, there's nothing wrong with English clothes. But you young fellows nowadays—you won't wear a stitch that wasn't made by a Dutchman."

I went down a steep hill to the Dutch quarter. It was as dazzling as the Venice Merceria, except that the stuff spilling out of the open shops was not silk but fine wool or fine linen, or an interweaving of both. Women sat in the cold sunshine and knitted woollen stockings; tailors, perched cross-legged by open windows, made up the stuff as fast as the weavers could weave it.

While a tailor was measuring me for a doublet, and a mantuamaker for a cloak, and a hatter for a hat, and a seamstress for six fine linen shirts; while I bargained with a knitter for the longest hose in her basket, these Dutch people were insinuating their questions. Had I, perhaps, just come into my inheritance? Without lying, I let them suppose that I was the son of a miserly father, who had always till now kept me poorly dressed. Then, to avoid further questioning, I asked them how they came to be in Colchester. Their answers were in broken English, but clear enough. "God bless Queen Elizabeth!" It was the Queen who had given them leave to live here, thirteen years before, when Haarlem fell to the Spaniards. They had been joined, since then, by compatriots fleeing from other towns. Each one had some story of a daughter raped, a father tortured, a baby snatched out of its mother's arms and killed— "for no cause, no reason, only devilry." This was why the miller's son had gone to fight the Spaniards.

Waiting for my clothes, I had to stay in Colchester three days. There was nothing to do but read the only two books the innkeeper possessed—Fox's *Book of Martyrs*, and the Protestant version of the Bible. Both were new to me; my mother and father had refused to have them in the house. Now I studied them eagerly, memorising the parts I would most likely have to answer.

On Saturday night I was distracted by the singing of drunken farmers. The words were shameful, but the tunes were lovely—some new to me, and some the very same which had enchanted the Italians. It was all I could do not to join in.

Sunday morning put me in a difficulty. "I feel . . . not quite myself," I told the innkeeper. This was an equivocation, not a lie. I did not feel myself, since I was in disguise. Nor was it a lie to add: "I can't go to church."

The innkeeper winked. "You stay in your room, sir. I'll tell the beadles you're ill. Do you think I haven't seen you, hour after hour, with your nose in the Bible? Bless you, sir, we're all of the same way of thinking here. I'd stay away from church myself, but, in my position, it wouldn't do to be known as a Puritan."

V I

ONCE I LOOKED LIKE a gentleman, I did not need an answer to every question. The questions were never asked. City watchmen, inn servants, even beadles, were timid and respectful. Small coins were greeted with grateful cries. "Thank you, sir. I'll drink your health, sir. You're a real gentleman."

Why, so I was. To all appearance I had lost my novice's humility, and had resumed the manners I was born to. When I cried out: "Open that gate, will you?" my voice resounded inside my head as the voice of my father. I had his pride of bearing and, besides, my own secret pride in my real mission. I felt myself exalted above other people, by far more than the height of a good horse.

Once I reached London, I soon found Lincoln's Inn Fields. There I did not ask the way, but looked at the sun, considered the time of day, and made up my mind which was the north-east corner. Sure enough, there was a turnstile, and a tall house beside it.

I knocked at the door. It was opened immediately. A voice whispered: "Are you looking for Father Sherwood?"

"That's right," I said.

"Then come in."

"Where shall I leave my horse?" I asked.

"We'll take good care of it."

Only when the door was closed behind me did the men surround me. A gag in my mouth, a knife-blade under my chin, a rope going round my wrists — all this was over before I felt it. The first clear thing was a voice — a rough, common voice, which I already knew from somewhere — saying: "What's his horse like?"

Someone answered: "A beauty!" Then laughter, and the first voice again: "The right horse for a Jesuit. They don't stint themselves, do they?" And other voices: "The King of Spain don't stint 'em." "Shall we see what he's carrying?"

They led me out of the dark hall, and up to a back bedroom, and I could see them. There were four of them. Three tied me to the bed, and took the gag out of my mouth. The one whose voice I thought I knew said: "Name?"

I said nothing. One raised his hand to hit me, but the questioner shook his head. "Not yet. There's no need. This'll be Paul Calverley, a gentleman by birth, six feet tall, fair-haired, missing from the English College in Rome since last November, seen arriving ten days ago at the Jesuit House in Rouen. Now, Paul, my lad, what are you carrying?" He undid my wallet and my money-belt.

There was more laughter when they counted out my money. "Where's your vow of poverty, then?" They made short work of the secret pocket; in an instant the letter was out. Father Parsons' new code they ridiculed as child's play. "I can read it from here," said the voice I knew. "Clear as print!" He read slowly: "I received a letter from Your Majesty' ... Your Majesty! This is another letter to the Queen of Scots!"

I cried out: "No, that's impossible!" — and then stopped. I had set my feet in a trap; I need not set my tongue there.

"Don't shout," said the questioner, "or I'll have to gag you again. When it's dark we'll take you to the Tower. You can shout as loud as you like in there. You may have cause." He smiled. "Now I'll return good for evil. You won't tell me your name, but I'll tell you mine. Topcliffe. Richard Topcliffe. What does that mean to you?"

"Nothing," I said. "And yet I know your voice."

"What! Have you and I met before? When?"

"I can't remember. But I know I've heard your voice."

He seemed really taken aback. "That's impossible. You've only just landed here. Look at you! New clothes, Dutch worsted, a Holland shirt, every stitch you're wearing made in the Low Countries . . .'"

I thought: he doesn't know there are Dutchmen in Colchester. Thank God! Those poor people won't be troubled for my sake. Not until afterwards did I wonder whether I ought to be sorry for heretics.

"No!" said Topcliffe. "You haven't been here before. If ever I saw a boy priest straight out of college . . . By the way, where did you land?"

The man who had been stabling my horse came back with my saddle bags. My beautiful new shirts (two still unworn) were pulled out amid more laughter. There was ribaldry over my shaving glass. "A naked Venus — just right for a priest!"

Topcliffe added: "That's Italian work. He couldn't have done better if he'd had it painted on a pole — 'I come from Rome.'"

Then they discovered the falconer's clothes. "A disguise! A Jesuitical disguise! This would be enough by itself to hang you! But praise the Lord! We have the letter as well."

I heard no more of the letter until the next day. The night I spent in the Tower, in quite a pleasant room. Topcliffe informed me that he was not greedy. He was keeping my horse as his perquisite, but he gave me back my money. Since I was a gentleman by birth, I was allowed to buy the comforts available to prisoners.

Before I lay down to sleep I prayed, and my prayers were answered. A calm disposition came to me, and I was able to consider what I ought to do.

After a good breakfast I was taken by two guards to a stately room, with tapestries on the walls and a carpet on the floor. Here I sat by the fire, until Topcliffe came in. He said: "Come on, Paul Calverley. Kneel!"

"To God?" I asked.

"To the Queen's privy councillor."

"Then I will kneel," I said, "out of respect for the Queen."

Since Topcliffe and his men were kneeling too, I knew that the person who now entered must be a great man. But which great man? He was very soberly dressed, and had a tired, unhealthy, bad-tempered face. The sight of me seemed to cause him some bodily pain. Mastering this, he sat down at a broad oak table, with a secretary beside him. I was made to stand facing him.

"You look well, Mr. Calverley," he said. "Have you been treated well?"

"Not badly, sir."

He told his secretary to make a note of that. "In case they pester us again in Parliament."

"But sir," I went on, "I have not been told the charge against me."

The great man nodded at his secretary, who then read out an indictment.

"That Paul Calverley, gentleman, of Yorkshire, born within this Kingdom of England after the feast of St. John the Baptist in the first year of the Queen's reign, and ordained priest before the last day of March in the twenty-eighth year of the Queen's reign, at Rome, beyond the seas, by authority derived from the See of Rome, thinking nothing of the laws and statues of this realm of England, and in no wise fearing the penalty contained in them, was on the said last day of March in London, in the parish of St. Andrew's, Holborn, in a traitor's way and as a traitor, carrying a letter addressed to the Queen of Scots."

"The last part is not true," I said.

"But you admit that you are Paul Calverley, a priest and a Jesuit?"

"I admit that." (In my calm state, the night before, I had

72

seen that it would be useless to deny it.) "I also admit that, if your new laws make it treason for me to enter my native country, to preach the faith of my ancestors, then by those laws you have power to put me to death. But of treason in the ordinary meaning of the term I am not guilty. I am a loyal subject of Queen Elizabeth. I know nothing of any letter to the Queen of Scots."

The great man sighed. "This is tedious. The letter was on you when you were taken. Isn't that so, Topcliffe?"

Topcliffe replied: "Yes, Sir Francis."

The great man must be Sir Francis Walsingham, the man who knew every thought in every head in Rome. Yet I was a Jesuit. I could face him. I said: "Sir, *a* letter was on me. A letter to a priest."

"To Richard Sherwood, otherwise known as Carleton. Yes. His name is mentioned in it. Your friend Parsons must have some particular grudge against him. And, I suppose, against you."

This was unexpected. I said nothing. Walsingham went on: "We have to do the same things over and over. Father Parsons despatched this very same letter last year, before he went to Rome, by another priest. We arrested that one a few days after he landed. He's an older man than you, but he looked equally foolish, when we read him the letter. Now, your Father Parsons, to make absolutely sure that this letter should come into our hands — and not knowing, I suppose, that his first messenger was taken — sends another copy with you. We knew that you'd been missing from the English College in Rome, ever since that scandal about the sodomy. We had your name and your description; we knew that Parsons must have sent you into our hands. He does that to any sodomite. Whether to punish him or to punish us . . ."

"I'm not a sodomite!"

He waved a weary hand. "That's not my concern. The point is — how urgently does Parsons want us to kill the Queen of Scots?"

"He wants *what*?"

Walsingham turned to the secretary. "We have to go through this again. Read it out."

The secretary read in a flat, monotonous voice: "I received a letter from Your Majesty . . . concerning your resolution to adventure your escape . . . Your Majesty . . . whose person is the principal and only foundation in deed that the Pope and the King of Spain and the Prince of Parma do rest upon . . . If Your Majesty's person were on this side the sea, or otherwise in security, you could not demand so abundant succours as you should have offered you in all things . . . If Your Majesty could think it possible and convenient to attempt your escape . . . it may be done with as little and less danger than to make your escape upon the arrival of forces . . ."

Here Walsingham broke in. "You understand that, Paul? 'The arrival of forces' means a Spanish invasion. We already know that the Queen of Scots is trying to escape. That does not in itself prove her guilty of treason against Queen Elizabeth. What this letter does is to involve her in Spanish plans to invade us."

I said: "Then it's impossible that Father Parsons could have written it."

Walsingham sighed. "Was there ever a man who wrote so many letters? And all in the same bustling, important style. The only change is that he alters the cipher now and then. But never so as to puzzle our Mr. Phillips" — he nodded at the secretary — "above an hour or two."

"I know his favourite words," Mr. Phillips explained. "God and the King of Spain. I could unravel the cipher from them, if I had to."

"But in this case there was no need," said Walsingham, "the key to the cipher having long since fallen into our hands."

I said: "Father Parsons cannot have written in favour of a Spanish invasion."

Walsingham said: "You must hear the rest of the letter."

There was another page about the proposed escape. Then: "For the payment of the 12,000 crowns to Your Majesty from Spain I will do what possible I may about it . . . I wrote before how the Prince of Parma had given commandment for payment thereof . . . The 1,000 crowns that I mentioned to Your Majesty in my last letter were sent to the King of Scots . . ."

Walsingham laughed. "Young King James has more sense than his mother. He takes this money from Spain to turn Catholic — and then stays Protestant."

Indeed, the next page of the letter complained of this. Then there was more about the Prince of Parma — the Spanish commander in the Low Countries, the man from whose cruelties the Dutch weavers had fled.

"No man has the commodity to despatch the enterprise so easily and quickly as the Prince of Parma . . ."

Here Walsingham interrupted the reading again. "*The enterprise* always means the invasion of England."

". . . In course of talk with the Prince of Parma when I was in the Low Countries, he asked my opinion in divers things, as whither I thought Your Majesty would most willingly go if you could escape . . . I presumed that you would trust no place sooner, if other occasions did concur, than the King of Spain's dominions, and where the Prince of Parma himself had the Government. Then he asked . . . whether you would marry again. Whereto I said that in that point I knew least. And when he still was questioning obscurely of such matter I, to draw from him some part of his meaning, said that, for Your Majesty's particular intent, I presumed not to know anything. Yet, for the general desire and wish of Catholics, I could assure him it should be no small contentation, if Your Majesty were in your royal seat — "

"He means, on the English throne," murmured Walsingham.

" — and provided of such a husband as His Highness was, for that would make a hope that it should be beneficial not only to England but to all Christendom. At that he smiled, and said that he pretended no such thing, but to do for Your Majesty only for good will, yet adding that he was not so mortified to the world but if all parties were agreed he could accept such a preferment with thankfulness."

I cried out: "This is incredible!"

"I agree," said Walsingham smoothly. "It is incredible that the Prince of Parma should want to marry a woman who murdered her second husband and repudiated her third. Particularly now that she's past forty, fat, with a double chin, and rheumatism. Even if he first invaded England, and placed her on the throne. No, I agree, that part of the conversation is invented. The question is, why did Parsons invent it?"

"He didn't!" I said.

"Then who did? You think I did? I am a clever fellow, but even I could not have invented what comes next."

Mr. Phillips continued his reading. "This only I touch by occasion of our present necessity. Your Majesty may do herein as you please, and use the knowledge thereof to yourself alone. If you thought it convenient, and could devise fit means whereby to cast out some hope or good liking that way upon the motion of some honourable friend in England, I think nothing in the world would so much set forward the Prince of Parma and hasten execution."

"Hasten the invasion, he means," put in Walsingham.

The letter continued: "For Your Majesty knoweth that every man nowadays, whatsoever he pretend, seeketh his own interest. But all this I leave to Your Majesty's consideration, craving pardon for my boldness in mentioning any such thing . . ."

"As well he might," Walsingham said. "You see what he is proposing? That she should not really agree to the marriage, but should hold it out as a bait to the Prince of Parma, so as to make him eager to invade us. If you'd read as many of Parsons' letters as I have, you'd know that he almost always proposes to the person he is addressing that the two of them should combine to deceive some third person. Oh, yes, and then the spiritual consolation! He can't end without that."

The reading continued: "I beseech Your Majesty to be of good cheer howsoever these things go, and to think this little part of Christ's cross which you bear, and have suffered these many years, to be the greatest benediction that possibly Your Majesty at God's hands could receive. Howbeit, for the good of the Church you and we must all pray and labour that you may be delivered from it . . ."

"Perhaps you think I invented the postscript?" said Walsingham.

The postscript was about the ways of passing letters to and fro. "There is a priest in London named Sherwood, otherwise now called Carleton (as I think) a man well experienced in matters who would serve very well (as I deem) for such an office if it should like Your Majesty to use him, and every Catholic in London can find him out."

"Indeed they could," said Walsingham. "And so could we. Was there ever a clearer invitation to us to arrest a man? When we had the first copy of this letter, last year, we took Sherwood the next day. He was not 'a man well experienced in matters'; he was a poor little fool, younger even than you. A gull to take bigger birds with! He's a common secular priest, not a Jesuit; I suppose Parsons had some grudge against him. Had Parsons any reason—apart from the sodomy—for handing you over to us?"

"He didn't do that!"

"And he didn't write that letter?"

"Never! I shall never believe he did."

Walsingham said: "Mr. Calverley, I have news for you. Parsons is in the pay of the King of Spain. Our agents have intercepted other letters, in which he urges that king to invade this country. Which he might well do, to seize it for himself. But not, I think, to put the Queen of Scots on the throne. If she were dead, the invasion would be more likely. Do you see now why Parsons urges her to incriminate herself?"

"I don't believe he does. I don't believe any of this."

"But you do know that the Spaniards are preparing to invade us?"

"I have heard that."

"And if they do land here, do you intend to fight for them, or for Queen Elizabeth?"

"I can't fight for anyone. I'm a priest."

"Of course, of course. And which side would you tell other people to fight for?"

"For Queen Elizabeth."

"A plain answer, from a Jesuit! But suppose that the Pope had blessed the banners of Spain. That would make a difference, eh?"

"No. I'd still be for my country and my Queen."

"Then you should be with us, in our English church."

"No. I'm a Catholic."

"How can you be?"

"There are Catholic princes who fight against the Pope. The present King of Spain did, when he was married to our Queen Mary. They were both good Catholics; they honoured the Pope as their spiritual head and father, but they fought against him as a temporal prince."

"An ingenious distinction!" Walsingham said.

"I am not the first one to make it. 'Render unto Caesar . . .'"

"And you take our Queen as your Caesar?"

"Yes. I accept her as my temporal ruler, but not as head of the church."

"The point is — you believe that Catholics ought to fight for her?"

"Yes."

"And be loyal to her?"

"Yes."

"Then will you show your loyalty by telling us who helped you to break the Queen's laws? Who landed you in this country? Who met you? What house did you hide in?"

I remembered Father Possevino, who had stood unmoved before the rage of Tsar Ivan. I could refuse to answer these questions. I still refused, when Walsingham repeated them two or three times.

"Perhaps," he said wearily, "you think I am asking you to change your religion. No! We don't employ 'comforters' to sit up all night with you, pestering you to recant. No, it's a matter of securing our shores against invasion. For our own

78

defence we must know where you landed. Surely you can see that?"

"Yes, I see it, but I can't answer your questions."

He turned to Topcliffe. "You find out!"

I had no doubt what this meant. From questioning me in a damp, cold cellar, to opening the door and letting me catch — as if by chance — a glimpse of the rack; from there to making me stand by the rack and see how it worked; then to the point of strapping me on it, and leaving me alone in utter darkness . . . I had foreseen every stage. I used the time they left me alone for prayer, and once again my prayers were answered. I was given grace to collect my thoughts.

What I thought was this. I was in the hands of men, not demons. They had good spies, but no supernatural knowledge. They could make mistakes. Topcliffe had still not guessed that my clothes came from Colchester. Moreover this forged letter, with which they had tried to bewilder and confuse me, was a poor piece of work. They had not been clever enough to make it sound like a real letter. How had Walsingham looked, at the moment when I told him that it was incredible? Though he had answered so readily, had there not been a flicker of surprise on his face? He must be used to simpler souls.

I heard footsteps. Topcliffe was returning with his men. I went once more through the prayer which was my protection. "Oh Lord God, Thou wilt not permit me to be tempted beyond my strength. The worst these men can do is kill me . . ."

It was not true. I understood, as they gathered about me, that it was not true. I feared one thing more than death — disfigurement. In these last months I had come to enjoy the daily sight of my own face in the shaving glass. I had enjoyed the look in the eyes of the village girls, when they dimpled and giggled at me. I had been proud of the splendid appearance I made, wearing my new clothes, and riding a good horse.

Horrified at this weakness, and yet glad that I had found it out in time, I sent up a hasty prayer.

Topcliffe was already asking: "Where did you land?"

Lord, if they turn me into a shambling, crooked creature, if

I can never again sit on a horse, if my golden hair goes white, Lord, help me to see that this does not matter!

Within me a demon was answering back. A crooked body was a high price to pay for protecting with my silence two smugglers, who had intended to rob me, and a heretic miller.

The actual beginning of the torture cleared my mind. The desperate pain in every joint showed me Topcliffe's desperate desire to know how I had landed, to seize any other priest who came that way.

For a minute or so my tormentors were shouting at me. What they said I did not hear; it was too much confused with my own cries. Then they stopped. The rack stopped. I heard the voice of Topcliffe, whispering into my ear: "You didn't know what was in that letter, did you? You've been fooled by the man who sent you."

"That's it!" I said. "That's it! That's when I heard your voice!" And as the torture began again I shrieked: "Kill me, then! I shall never tell you anything!"

I came to in bed – the same comfortable bed in which I had spent the night. An old woman was bending over me, bathing my brow. I raised my head and saw Topcliffe looking at me. I knew I had something important to say to him.

"You were in Rome. It was your voice I heard in the English College in Rome."

"Not me!" Topcliffe said. "Never out of England, thank God!"

"But it was the same voice, the same whisper, the same words. 'You didn't know what was in that letter, did you? You've been fooled by the man who sent you.' I heard you say it the summer before last, in Rome."

"He's raving!" Topcliffe said. Then, to the old woman mopping my brow: "Is he in a fever?"

She felt my cheeks, listened to my heart's beating, and sniffed at my breath. "You won't get no sense out of him today," she said.

Topcliffe told her: "You're a laundress, not a doctor."

"Very well, sir! You ask Dr. Larkin."

Topcliffe grunted and left the room. The old woman ran to the door, made sure there was nobody outside it, and bolted it fast. She plumped down on her knees beside the bed, and whispered: "Father, give me your blessing!"

I looked into her face — an English face, not rosy now, nor sunburned, but carrying in its wrinkles the memory of roses and sunshine. Her eyes were filled with reverence for me. I was glad with all my heart that I could look into those eyes, that I had kept my faith intact, that I had not been confused either by torture or by clumsy forgeries.

I sat up. I still had on the shirt and breeches I had been wearing when they put me on the rack. Though I ached all over, I was able to get out of bed and stand up. This appeared to me a miracle; it was as if her faith had made me whole.

I blessed her, and then thanked her for having protected me from further torment. "Am I really feverish?" I asked.

"No; but you will be, if they get their hands on you again. I've seen a young man die of a festering wound they gave him, and then they gave it out he'd killed himself. Quick! Back to bed! I'll give you medicine to make you seem worse than you are."

Before I took the medicine I asked her: "Where was Topcliffe the summer before last?"

"Here. Where else? But he's a devil; he could be in two places at once."

The medicine must have been mainly opium; it made me drowsy. Dr. Larkin seemed to be deceived; I heard him, through my stupor, telling Topcliffe that I could not be put on the rack again that day.

I never was put on the rack again. A few days later they rowed me up the river a mile or so, to the prison called the Clink. As I came up the water steps I was aware of a stir, with faces appearing at barred windows. I was led into a courtyard, and a crowd of people, who seemed to be visiting the prison, came pressing round me. Women's voices called out, asking me how I had stood the racking. Did it hurt me to walk? I told them; not very much.

Again, my money got me a good room. I was visited there by a fellow-prisoner, whose face I knew.

"Christopher Bagshaw!" I said. "Did you become a priest, then, after all?"

He laughed. "A priest, and a doctor of Theology. They made me that at Padua University, after I left Rome. Did you know I was a doctor of Theology at Oxford, long ago? I said to them at Padua: 'That doesn't count; it was heretic theology.' 'Not at all,' they said. 'Not at all; the course of study is the same.' So they questioned me, to make sure I was a good Catholic; they got the local bishop to ordain me priest; and then they accepted me with no trouble at all. You should have seen old Parsons' face, when I turned up at Rouen with my doctorate! I said to him: 'Do you want me to hang about here, or am I to go to England?' He asked me – was I willing to become a Jesuit? 'No,' I said. 'I'm a simple priest; that's enough.' So he was in a dilemma. There's never enough priests willing to go to England. If he rejected me, and I appealed to the Pope, how could he justify himself?"

I asked: "Why wouldn't you become a Jesuit?"

"Why, for that very reason. So that I could appeal to the Pope, like any other Catholic. You can't do that, Paul. You've sworn obedience to your superior, whoever that is – Parsons, I suppose. I wasn't walking into that particular trap. I walked into the other one, it's true – the one that Parsons made for me."

"What do you mean?"

"To think that I could be so simple, after all the years I've known him! He's hated me ever since we were both at Oxford. Well, just as I was leaving, he came to me and begged me to forget all our past quarrels. I swear to you, Paul, he was weeping – real tears! He said he hadn't believed I really meant to go to England, to risk martyrdom for the Faith. Could I forgive him? Of course I forgave him – what else could I do? More and more tears – he was weeping still, when he gave me that confounded letter."

I did not ask – what letter? I did not want to know.

"Spiritual consolation!" Christopher Bagshaw said. "A message to a brother priest in danger of giving way. You know, I suppose, that at least a dozen priests have turned Protestant?"

"No! Impossible!"

"Queen Elizabeth has the sense to make it easy for them. A good living in her church, a pleasant vicarage, a plump, rosy English wife — some of our boys can't resist. Well, here was one just wavering, not yet beyond salvation — how could I refuse to take him a letter? Do you know, I was fool enough to sew it into my shirt? The two ruffians who brought me to land stripped me of everything else, and I actually fought them for my shirt. They tore it, and then decided it wasn't worth taking. That's all I had left — the shirt and the letter inside — when I found my way to the mill."

"The tide-mill? Was it a tide-mill?"

"How do I know what sort of a mill? The miller was a good fellow; he gave me some clothes, and five shillings — a fortune to him. I wish to God I could repay him. But I'd never find the place again."

I said: "I could find it again."

"Oh, did you come that way too? A bit careless of the Jesuit fathers in Rouen, don't you think, to send us there? It almost looks as if they meant us to be taken."

"No! Christopher, for God's sake, you mustn't say that! Walsingham said that."

"Yes, he said it to me too. Of course, in my case it was obvious. Parsons directed me to a house which was already in their hands."

"He can't have known."

"I suppose you think he didn't know what was in his own letter. 'If Your Majesty were in your royal seat . . .'"

"That letter was forged!"

"Nobody could forge a letter from old Parsons. There isn't another man in the world with such a twisted mind."

"Christopher, don't be blinded by your feelings about him. Walsingham forged that letter. He didn't even forge it very

83

well. And he couldn't trouble himself to forge two different letters for you and for me. He read the same one to both of us."

"Parsons always writes his letters twice over. I've seen him do that at Rouen. So as to make sure that one copy gets through, he says. Or is it so as to make sure that he lands more than one person in trouble?"

"Christopher, that letter was forged."

"Oh, if you keep saying so, it must be true."

"But I *know*. Listen! In Rome — " I whispered this part " — in Rome, Sir Francis Englefield said that the English Catholics were to blame for their own plight, because they wouldn't support a Spanish invasion. And I said — "

"Oh, Paul, Paul, I know what you said. You said — and I'm sure you meant it — that this wasn't the way; that foreign soldiers could never implant the Faith in the hearts of our English people."

"If you know what I said, you must know that Father Parsons agreed with me. He told Englefield that I was right."

"And then, since Englefield had been talking this treason. Parsons had no more to do with him?"

I hesitated. Christopher laughed. "Come, Paul — no Jesuit equivocation. Five minutes after this pretended disagreement, weren't they as good friends as ever?"

"I think . . . I think people make allowances for Englefield, because he's embittered. The Queen has taken his estate, although he made it over to his nephew."

"Made it over to his nephew! Is there a country in the world where such a legal quibble would save a traitor's goods? Englefield can hardly say he needs the money. He has a very generous pension from the King of Spain."

"And yet, when he was advising me about my journey, he said: 'We'd all rather sleep among heretics than Spanish troops.'"

Christopher laughed. "He thinks, when his golden day comes, he won't be sleeping among the soldiers. He'll be in a silken tent, advising the Prince of Parma which of us ought to be hanged. And Parsons beside him."

"No! Not Father Parsons!"

"Then why is he so thick with Englefield?"

"Well . . . Englefield is good at planning disguises. That may be why Father Parsons makes use of him."

"If anybody was made use of, Paul, my boy, it was you. Parsons plays this little comedy in front of every priest he thinks of sending to England. With various people taking the Englefield part. If the priest agrees with Englefield, if he looks forward eagerly to a Spanish invasion, Parsons will see to it that he isn't caught. That is, not at once. Parsons needs one or two people at liberty in England, to carry out his plans. But the innocents, the lads like you, are sent straight into the lion's mouth. Because you can declare — can go to the gallows declaring — that you have nothing to do with any plot for the invasion of England. What an effect that has on simple people! To see a young man protesting with his dying breath his utter innocence of treason — what can make Elizabeth's Government look more cruel? What can make its laws look more completely unjust? Which, alas — in view of Parsons' real aims — they are not."

"Christopher! You're saying that the Government is right."

"Not in everything. No; they should never have made the Mass illegal; they should never have compelled people to go to their church. When Elizabeth first came to the throne, she ought to have declared a general toleration."

"Toleration? You mean a complete confusion, like they have in Bohemia?"

"It'll come to that, and the sooner the better. What good have we ever done ourselves, by burning Protestants? Have you read their famous Book of Martyrs?"

"Yes. I thought it was mostly lies."

"Why? Haven't you seen Protestants put to death, in the Campo de' Fiori? Don't they die bravely? Don't you think their friends take the same pride in them that we do in our martyrs? Look at that place where we landed, you and I! Queen Mary burned more people in Essex than anywhere else, bar London, and what's the result? Everybody you speak to seems to be some sort of Puritan."

"Yes, but there's no peace among them. There's no two can agree about what they do believe."

"There's our chance, if we knew how to take it! When people are tired of this wrangling, tired of the quibbling over mis-translated fragments of the Bible, we can offer them the peace of the universal Church. We're better educated than the Protestants, more active. We haven't any wives to tie us down. We're prepared to ride a thousand miles, if at the end there's one soul to be saved. Toleration would give us our chance."

"Then that must be why the Government won't allow it."

"No. There are men within this Government who long for toleration. What prevents it is that we've been working for Spain."

"I haven't."

"You think you haven't. I thought the same. And so did all our martyrs. But you and I and they have been working for Parsons, who belongs heart and soul to the King of Spain."

"I still don't believe that."

"Oh, Paul, Paul! Where do you think the money comes from? The money for the Seminary at Rheims, for the English College at Rome—the money that was given you at Rouen?"

"It's the contributions of the English Catholics."

"I thought you came into this country the same way as I did. I thought you had found a certain difficulty, in landing unobserved. Well, it's quite as difficult to leave the country. How do you imagine that large sums of money could regularly be transported out of England? We do collect from the faithful, but we spend that money here. Don't you know by now what it costs to live in prison? It's all our friends can do to keep us prisoners comfortable, and provide good horses and clothes for those priests who are still at liberty. Because it's impossible to stay at liberty, unless you go about like a gentleman. I was in continual trouble, wearing the miller's old clothes. Always dodging behind hedges to avoid being arrested as a vagrant. It took me a week to walk to London."

I had been all this time looking for weak points in what he said. Now I thought I had spotted one.

"When they arrested you," I asked, "did they ask you how you'd landed?"

"Yes, of course."

"Did you tell them?"

"No."

"Then why didn't they put you on the rack?"

"They were going to. But some of my old friends from Oxford interceded for me. Besides, when anybody's racked, although it's done in secret, although the walls of the Tower can stifle any cries, it's known all over London within the hour."

I thought of the pious laundress, and said: "Yes, I can see how that might happen."

"That's probably why they didn't rack you again. There are one or two Members of Parliament who make trouble for the Government."

"Walsingham said that. But how can it be true? Surely the Members of Parliament are all Protestants."

"Paul, you're in England now. There are people here who believe it's wrong to torture anyone, even those who differ from them in religion. Besides, torture is against the laws of England. Some of these people in Parliament argue that therefore it ought not to happen. Not even in the Queen's own prisons."

"There may be one or two people who think so, but they can't be very strong."

"We could make them stronger. We Catholics could be working with them, not against them. Paul, there are people here who hate what they do to us. Topcliffe, I know, enjoys using the rack. But I don't believe that Walsingham enjoys using Topcliffe. He thinks it's his duty to his country."

"No!" I said. "They're both devils."

"Nobody we meet here on earth is a devil. Wicked men, maybe, but they still are men."

I said: "I'm not sure of that." And I told him the story of the voice I had heard in Rome.

He asked me gently: "Are you sure, Paul? You were very weak then. You'd been fasting a long time."

"I was fasting; I was delirious; Father Agazzari told me afterwards that nobody had really whispered in my ear. But there are truths we can perceive only when we're weak from fasting, else why do the saints fast? I believe that what I heard was a threat from a devil."

"Are you so sure," said Christopher, "that it was not a warning from an angel?"

VII

I THOUGHT I COULD be sure of that. It was clearly no accident that my captors had placed me in the same prison as a man who talked like this, and had allowed him such easy access to me.

Then I found that every Catholic in London had easy access to me. The keeper and warders of the Clink were the pleasantest men who ever took bribes. The Clink stands on the south bank of the river, and everyone who has a penny for a boatman comes to it by water. Any great man from city or court can be seen slowly approaching in his own barge. Our warders always gave us ample warning; we had time to hide away the vestments, the folding altars, the wafers and wine, with which we said Mass every day in the storeroom we used as a chapel. By the time the great man arrived all our visitors would be gone, and we would be locked in our separate rooms, the warders jangling the keys as busily as if we had not every one a duplicate.

These inspections were not frequent, and at all other times we carried on our pastoral work, hearing confessions, preaching sermons and giving advice. Catholics were flocking to London then. In a village it was impossible to avoid notice if you did not go to church. In London it was easy, particularly if you changed your lodgings from time to time. Puritans came to London for the same reason, and many cases of conscience were put to us by Catholics who found themselves living next door to Puritans — perhaps even in the same house. Was it right for a Catholic to make a pact with a Puritan, that neither would denounce the other for staying away from church? Christopher said yes; the more allies we had in our fight for freedom of conscience, the better. They had not prepared us for this question in Rome; nobody had imagined there were so many Puritans in England. I argued as Christopher did, and tried to seem calm and certain, because the Catholics looked so confidently to us priests. In the daytime we never hinted at any disagreements among ourselves.

But after sunset, when the last visitor had left, and the gates had been bolted, our disputes began. There were six of us priests, but I was the only Jesuit — almost the only one in England. Father Weston, who had come to England eighteen months before, was nominally my superior. But I could not consult him; he was hiding in some country house, having become too famous for his own safety, because he cast evil spirits out of madmen. The other priests asked me whether I knew him. I had to reply that I did not; while I was in Rome he had been attending a college in Spain.

"In Spain!" said Christopher. "And he wasn't captured when he landed. You see?"

Three of the other secular priests agreed with him. I had one unexpected ally — Richard Sherwood. He said: "Walsingham tried to make me believe that Father Parsons delivered me into his hands. But I don't believe that. I never will. Just because I had words with Father Parsons, before I set out for England — "

I asked him: "What words did you have?"

"Oh, just the usual things . . . Forgive me, Paul, but everybody says you Jesuits have made yourselves a church within the Church; you obey your General Aquaviva, not the Pope; you think yourselves a cut above us ordinary priests, and try to give us orders.'

"You said all that to Father Parsons?"

"Yes, because he said that when I reached England I ought to seek out this Jesuit — Father Weston — and take my orders from him. I said I didn't see why. In fact, I was cheeky. But Father Parsons wasn't angry — truly not. He only looked at me in a sort of a grieved way."

"I know that look," muttered Christopher.

"And he said: 'So that's how it seems to you, Richard, is it?' Then he explained how hard things are in England, with no bishop to guide us, and the weaker priests going over to the enemy. We shouldn't be too proud to take advice from people with more experience. Well, I could see that was reasonable. We made friends. When I landed here, though, I couldn't consult Father Weston; it was too dangerous even to go looking for him. Unless you know some nobleman personally, and can hide in his house, the only safe place is London."

"If London is so safe," Christopher asked him, "why do you think you were arrested the day after I was?"

"It was the neighbours. I'm sure it was the neighbours. People have a reward, if they lay information against us."

I said: "All of us here were taken at one time or another. Even you, Christopher, can't blame every arrest on Father Parsons."

The other three priests round the table said that was the man they did blame. Each one had some story of the carelessness, the rank bad advice of the Jesuit Fathers at Rouen (who acted, as a rule, under Parsons' direction). Wearing the wrong clothes, making for the wrong places, they had all three been arrested within a few hours of landing. I could only reply that their complaints had now reached Rome. "These things," I said, "are being put right."

"Who by?" asked Christopher.

I did not want to answer: "By Sir Francis Englefield." So I said: "The Jesuit Fathers in Rouen were most careful how they dressed me. They called in a great friend of theirs, Monsieur Delahaye—he's in the service of the Duke of Guise —and he agreed I looked exactly like a falconer."

"Did English people think so?" Christopher asked.

"Mostly they did. Only the miller knew I was a priest. He said it was in my face."

Everyone burst out laughing. But I went on: "He said it was in Christopher's face, too."

"In mine?" said Christopher. "Why, what's in my face? Let's have your shaving mirror, Paul."

He looked a long time at his blunt, short nose, at his worn cheeks, at his brown beard beginning to turn grey. He said: "It's that sad stare. We all have it, even when we smile. The smile of a priest is not like the smile of a man."

A fortnight after my first coming to the Clink, as I was saying Mass, I heard the door creak open. Over my shoulder I saw three strangers; a man, a woman and a young girl, all wearing black. There was no room for them to sit down, but they stood reverently at the back, keeping their eyes fixed on me.

I was put out. Christopher, whose turn it was that morning to stand guard at the door, was supposed not to admit anyone whose face we did not know. These people might be spies. But I was now too far in the sacred mysteries to break off.

When I held up the Host, I thought I heard sobbing somewhere behind me. Later, when I turned towards my congregation, I saw that the woman and the young girl were weeping. The three strangers did not leave with the others. It seemed that they wanted to speak privately to me. The man was weeping more quietly than the women, but more desperately. I thought I understood why. "Is it very long," I asked, "since you heard Mass?"

The woman cried out: "Don't you know us, Paul?"

At the sound of that voice I fell on my knees and asked a blessing from my father and mother.

I would have known them before, I think, if it had not been

for the young girl. I knew I had no sister. "This is Anne," my father explained. "The daughter of Margaret Clitheroe."

I had not heard the name before, but I let that go, since I now had to answer my mother's questions. Yes, I was well; I had plenty to eat; I was fully recovered from the rack. Moreover, I had not been put on trial, and, therefore, could not yet be hanged.

Here my father put a word in, saying that before I was tried he meant to seek out some old friends at court.

"But going to court costs money," I said. "And you've been ruined by the fines."

He reassured me. The fines they were ordered to pay for not going to church would have ruined them. But some great Catholic landowners had appealed to the Privy Council, declaring their loyalty to the Queen, and saying that it was not in Her Majesty's own interests to ruin so large a part of her subjects. The Privy Council then made an agreement with a number of Catholic gentlefolk, that they should pay a moderate amount each year, and not be further troubled by the law. But the Catholics were forbidden to mention this in public, or put it in a letter. That was why I had not heard.

"Thank God, we are not short of anything," my mother said. "But you, Paul? Are you really comfortable here?"

"It's better than a good inn."

"How kind your friend is!" my mother went on. "The one keeping watch by the door. He seems very fond of you."

The thought of Christopher being fond of me disturbed me so much that I said what we never said to lay people. "Don't . . . don't say too much to him."

"Oh, Paul, shouldn't we have trusted him? But surely he's a priest? I gave him the basket — the basket of jellies and jams I brought you."

"That's all right; you can trust him with food. Or money. He's in charge of everything we collect from the faithful; he buys the provisions for our common table, pays the warders their bribes . . . I'm sure he's honest that way. Only he talks as if — well, as if the Queen didn't want to persecute us."

"A good many people think so," my father said. "That was why we went to Margaret Clitheroe's trial. We thought that if we persuaded the judge to some delay, long enough to appeal to the Queen, we could save poor Margaret."

"Yes, the Queen would have reprieved her," my mother put in. "Everyone said so. That was why Margaret's enemies hurried it on so fast."

This was all new to me. It had happened about the time I landed in England. Margaret Clitheroe, the wife of a butcher at York, had been accused of harbouring a priest, and had refused to plead either guilty or not guilty. The penalty for this refusal — as the judge warned her seven times — was to be pressed to death under heavy stones.

"But she still wouldn't plead," my mother said. "Because, if she'd said either guilty or not guilty, there would have been a trial. Then Anne here, and the younger children, would have been forced to give evidence. And what could they say? If they'd said there never was a priest in the house, they'd have had the sin of perjury on their souls. And if they'd been truthful they would have condemned their own mother to death. Rather than put such a choice before them, our poor Margaret thought it better to die without a trial."

"They would not let her see me before she died," Anne said. "Or even write to me. But she sent me her shoes and stockings, to signify that I should follow in her footsteps."

"And so you do!" said my mother. "As good a girl as ever walked. Paul, Anne wants to go to France, and be a nun. When we heard you were taken, we were already setting out for London, to ask some people we know if they could put Anne aboard a ship. But they say the ships are too carefully searched nowadays."

On this question I consulted the other priests. They said there was a house of English nuns at Louvain. But Anne could not go there as things were. One man alone might be smuggled out of the country. But a young girl would need some sort of a bodyguard; whatever foreign port she landed in would probably be full of soldiers.

Christopher found words to comfort Anne. "It may be God's will you should stay here. There are good works for you to do in London. We priests in the Clink are comfortable, but there are Catholics in other prisons, where the warders can't be bribed. We've been hearing of people packed into cellars with common thieves, fed on crusts and foul water, made to work the treadmill, dying of jail fever—all for want of powerful friends. We need more people, not only to collect money, but to run up and down, finding out which great men have the power to help. If we know how to ask, we may find help any-where—even among Protestants."

"Oh, that's true!" my mother said. "Do you know, they sent a Puritan preacher to Margaret, to beg her to change her mind. She told him to get out of her sight. And yet it was this very Puritan who came into court and pleaded for her."

My father added: "He said every word that I had meant to say, if they had let me speak."

"Yes, and it was his doing," my mother said, "that they let her have ten days to ask for a reprieve. It wasn't long enough; we couldn't reach the Queen."

"The Council of the North refused her a reprieve," said Anne. "They told us that was good enough; the Council represented the Queen in our parts. They killed her directly after. They told her she would have to strip naked first; she was more afraid of that than of dying."

"But in the end they never put her to that shame," said my mother. "The prison women stood round her while she stripped, and when she lay down they hid her with a big wooden door, before the men put the weights on her. They say she died so soon, it was as if God put out His hand to take her."

Anne's lips opened a little, as if to drink in comfort from my mother's words. I was aware of something long known to me in her look. And yet I could not have seen her before I left England; or, if I had, she must have been a child. She was even yet very young. Above her serious brow her hair was parted smoothly, but little single hairs escaped, curling and shining where the light fell on them. For all her grief, her face was bright with country air. I could see why Christopher thought she might touch the hearts of people who could not be bribed.

She was in fact successful in this, and it did her good. Helping the poorest prisoners, Anne felt more close to her martyred mother. I did not see grief get the better of her until a fortnight later, when she and my parents were in the courtyard with me, and a new prisoner was brought in. He started at the sight of Anne, but said nothing. Anne staggered into my mother's arms.

Yet she did not faint. She was able to walk into my room, where she sat down and gave way to passionate weeping. My mother told me: "That was Father Mush."

"Who?"

"The priest poor Margaret was hiding. She smuggled him out of her house while the searchers were at the door."

"It wasn't his fault," Anne said. "I'll have to tell him." She jumped up. "I must see him at once, to tell him it wasn't his fault."

"Wait!" I said. "Christopher will arrange things; we shall all be able to see him presently. But you must give over crying, or he'll think you *are* blaming him."

"I'll stop crying; I will. It's only—to think that mother saved him, and now he's been arrested all the same."

"It is not the same," said my father. "If he'd been arrested in York, he would certainly have been hanged. We know what sort of people govern the North. Whereas in London he has good hopes of life. As they tell me Paul has." (For my father had been constantly at court, and had been well fed with promises.)

When we were able to see John Mush, he said: "You do understand, Anne? If I had given myself up, it would not have helped your mother. It would only have proved that she had in fact been hiding a priest."

"She knew that," Anne said. "She said in court that she was glad and proud of all she did for you."

John Mush had already begun to write the story of Margaret

Clitheroe. He made notes of what Anne and my father and mother told him about the trial. Prison, he said, was a good place to write; there was no fear of being suddenly taken away.

All of us in the Clink were now passing our days in the work we loved best. My only sorrow was that I could not form a choir. A Mass with music would have been heard in the street outside. In other ways our prison was our home. My father's friends at court assured him that the Government's one wish was to leave all us priests as we were, provided that we made no attempt to escape.

"You see?" said Christopher Bagshaw (arguing, as usual, at night, when our visitors had gone.) "It seems a fair bargain. We're in prison, but we're doing more pastoral work than if we were riding the country from end to end."

"Yes," I said, "but all our visitors' names are taken. The Government could arrest every one of them if it liked."

"But it won't like," said Christopher, "unless we do something foolish."

"Unless the Jesuits do," John Mush put in.

I bristled. Christopher quickly said: "Don't be angry, Paul. John didn't mean to offend you. He is bitter because of this poor woman who died for hiding him. He feels it was all caused by meddling in politics."

"But she didn't meddle in politics."

"That's just it," replied John Mush. "Mrs. Clitheroe didn't, but other people did. Why are things worse for Catholics in the North? Because they had an armed rising there, and a plot to make the Queen of Scots our queen. You're too young to remember that, Paul."

"I do remember. I was about eight. My father wouldn't join the rising; he said that the Queen of Scots was no sort of a leader for Catholics."

"Your father's a sensible man. That woman married her Bothwell by Protestant rites, not to mention other matters. And yet some Catholics were silly enough to fight for her. Then, just as things were settling down again, just as the persecution was easing, the Spaniards landed in Ireland. And with the Spaniards an English priest, a great friend of Parsons, called Sanders. I know the Irish are Catholics. But what Englishman can think of them as anything but savages? Even Edmund Campion wrote a book to prove that God intended the English to rule over Ireland. And when the Spaniards were there, inciting the Irish to rise — that was the moment Campion and Parsons chose to land here."

I protested. "Father Campion and Father Parsons had no idea what the Spaniards were going to do in Ireland. Their own instructions told them never to mention politics."

"You've left something out," said John Mush. "Their instructions told them never to mention politics *unless they were quite sure of their company.*"

"No! I don't believe that!"

"Haven't you learned anything yet? Are you as innocent as on the day you were delivered straight into Walsingham's hands?"

"Don't say that! Some of us are captured; some stay free. You were free yourself until the other day."

"I was free," said John Mush, "because — God forgive me — I took the side of the Jesuits, when they were plotting to win control of the English College in Rome. Parsons told me I was 'almost a Jesuit', which is the highest praise he can bestow on any secular priest. He made sure that a trustworthy captain brought me here, and that I knew a trustworthy hiding-place."

"You're not the only one. Father Weston is free still."

"Weston's a Jesuit. He landed here with a lay brother called Emerson. Parsons had given this Emerson a big box to carry. Pious books, he said. When the Queen's men opened that box, they surrounded Emerson, and forgot to hunt for Weston."

"Why? What was in the box?"

"Oh, a few hundred copies of a pamphlet Parsons wrote, called *Leicester's Commonwealth.* About the Earl of Leicester being a murderer and, it's broadly hinted, the Queen's lover. Just the thing to make life easier for English Catholics."

"I've never heard of such a pamphlet."

"No. No more had Mrs. Clitheroe."

98

"But what makes you think," I asked, "that it really was by Parsons? The only pamphlet of his that I've read was one asking for liberty of conscience."

Christopher smiled. "That's a pretty phrase. The people burned in the Campo de' Fiori would be glad to know that Parsons favours liberty of conscience."

John turned to him, saying passionately: "You can laugh at that? I can't. When I think of old Parsons, writing his pamphlets, finding one phrase to please one person, another to please the next; when I think of him living in safety, letting his fancy conquer great kingdoms . . . He's like a real conqueror in one thing; he leaves real mangled bodies everywhere."

I started up from the table. Christopher caught me in his arms and held me back. He rebuked John Mush for offending such a good hard-working priest as myself. "He won't believe what you say of Parsons – and why should he, when he's had no proof? Paul is as innocent as . . . as Richard Sherwood here." Christopher smiled. Not wanting to quarrel, I did not call it a pitying smile.

From that time forward my fellow-priests were careful not to utter a word I could object to. This put a constraint on my own tongue. I could not speak to anyone about the things which troubled me most.

When my parents came to see me I talked about the past; the happy childhood they had given me, my journeys after they had sent me overseas. I did not speak of Parsons, but found comfort in describing my undoubted heroes, the gentle Father Campion, the princely Father Possevino.

"But, Paul," my mother said, "why did your Father Possevino prevent the Russians from going to their own church?"

"Because it was heretical."

"But it was theirs, Paul. Isn't that what we say to the Protestants? We're sticking to *our* Church, the Church of our fathers. That was what Edmund Campion said to his judges. 'In condemning me you condemn your own ancestors.' And yet you expected these Russians to condemn their ancestors."

"*Their* ancestors were mistaken. Why, in their church, only monks and bishops are celibate. Parish priests are allowed to marry."

"I wish they were in our Church!" my mother said. "After all, that's the strongest point the heretics have against us. These terrible scandals — "

My father, seeing my face, warned her not to say any more. But I was not, as he thought, angry with her. I was dashed by my own sudden recollection that, by keeping the Russians out of their own church, I had delivered them into the clutches of whores.

I became aware of glances interchanged between my father and mother. Something apart from the subject of our conversation was weighing on their minds. I asked them whether it was money.

They reassured me. My father said that, to his own surprise, he had not given a single bribe at court. There were plenty of secret Catholics, who thought it a pious duty to help any priest in trouble.

"I was right, by the way," my father said. "If they'd known of it in time, they could have saved Margaret Clitheroe. Some of them are great men in the Government. They all go to church, of course; they have to, to keep their places near the Queen."

"If them, why not us?" my mother muttered. My father frowned at her, and shook his head.

I said: "It's mortal sin for *any* Catholic to enter the Queen's church. We were told in Rome to make no exceptions; nobody can be absolved, even if he argues that by appearing in church he can save the lives of other Catholics."

"It's lucky for you they don't all obey you," my mother said.

"Mother, it's not a question of obeying *me*. This is the teaching of the Church. And I remember, when I was a child, you yourself — "

"Oh yes, yes, I know! We were so young then, so sure of everything! And now the young priests are so sure, the Jesuits!"

"That's enough!" my father told her. But she went on:
"Paul, I know that you're a Jesuit, and in prison for it, and
perhaps going to be martyred. That's why your father thinks
I shouldn't say . . ."

She melted into tears. I turned in surprise to my father.
He muttered: "Well, you'd better hear it all now. The fact is,
Paul, there's been a great deal said about the Jesuits. Among
good Catholics, I mean. I don't care what the heretics may say.
I know you're not in league with Spain, or smuggling letters to
the Queen of Scots. But when a young fellow straight from
college comes into a Catholic home, and tells the wife to disobey the husband — "

"There's warrant for that in the Gospels," I said.

"There's warrant for *anything* in the Gospels, Paul, if you
listen to Puritans. But Catholics are people who want to live
as . . . as people always have lived. Loyal to their Queen and
country, the children obeying the parents, the wife obeying
the husband . . ."

"Or talking him round," murmured my mother.

"Yes, we know you get the better of us in the end. But not
by shaming us in public! This is what happened, Paul, to a
man we know. A Catholic gentleman, a Justice of the Peace,
able to prevent the harrying of Catholics anywhere within his
district. In order to keep his position he goes to the Queen's
church at Christmas and Easter. I wouldn't do that; your
mother wouldn't do it; but he does. He knows it's a sin; he
confesses it to an old priest from Queen Mary's time, who
gives him absolution. His wife has to appear in church beside
him; that's the custom; he'd be in trouble if she didn't. So the
old priest gives her absolution too. Now this Jesuit comes and
persuades the wife that she must never set foot in a church
again. She's to disobey her husband, and in public! The
husband orders the Jesuit out of the house. He refuses to go.
If he steps outside, he says, he'll be arrested. 'And then my
blood will be on your head.' Now, Paul, what's my friend to
do?"

"Make friends with his wife. Stop going to church. Resign his position as J.P."

"You've left something out," said my father. "This Jesuit said what you say — and then he added: 'Turn that old priest out of doors! He deserves it, for letting you go to church all these years!' A man of seventy, Paul! A man who's been tutor to my friend and his children. 'He's only a common hedge-priest,' the Jesuit said. Well, that did some good, after all. Because, when the wife heard it, *she* turned against the Jesuit. So he had to move out, and the couple were friends again."

"What became of the Jesuit?"

"He was arrested, but not hung. He's in Wisbech Castle."

Seeing how much I was cast down, my mother hastily said that not all Jesuits deserved their reputation. Some were different. She knew I was different . . . Intending to comfort me, my mother added: "I shall never think of you as a real Jesuit."

VIII

IN JULY THERE WAS a general exodus of country Catholics. I begged my parents to leave London too. I knew how uneasy it would make them both, to be away from our home farm at harvest-time. They had done all they could for me, and I was content. Only I had to be careful not to repeat the words: *Our home farm at harvest-time.* I could not say them in a steady voice.

To my great relief, I did at last persuade them to go. Or Anne Clitheroe persuaded them. She would write, she said, if any harm threatened me. She would be always near me; she was not likely to leave London.

Mr. Foscue, the Catholic with whom Anne was lodging, was, like her own father, a butcher, but in a bigger way. He used to send shiploads of bacon and salt pork to France. Her hope had been that he would send her too. But he said that every day it became less possible; Walsingham had replaced the old bribe-taking searchers with men who worked from pure Protestant zeal.

However, Mr. Foscue was glad to let Anne stay in his house.

He and his wife and daughters told me that she had brought them a blessing — perhaps the greatest blessing that can fall on any house. In her presence it was impossible to quarrel.

The only fault they found in her was recklessness. If none of the Foscue family had time to go with her, she would run into the worst London prisons, quite alone.

"But nobody does me any harm!" said Anne. Once she came to me laughing. "The thieves in Bridewell made such a to-do! They began beating one of their own companions, and I told them to stop, and they said the man would have to ask my pardon on his knees. And he did! He knelt in front of me and said he was very sorry he'd used a bad word when I was near by."

"Oh, Anne! Was it a very bad word?"

"That's what makes me laugh! I hadn't even heard it!"

Whenever Anne came near me I was calm; in her I saw the essential part of our Faith. Whatever differences we priests might have among ourselves were lesser things . . . And yet, somehow, I could not mention them to Anne. So I never spoke to her quite freely.

I should have been able to speak more freely to Richard Sherwood, since he was on my side. He agreed with me that Father Parsons had been horribly maligned. "If I can get abroad again," he told me, "I'll join the Jesuits. Because people like you, Paul — so firm, so *undoubting* — you are the real soldiers of Christ." Why did this admiration make me uneasy?

If only I had said more to Richard at the start, I might have been better able to deter him on that day, towards the end of July, 1586, when he came to me and made his confession. We all confessed to one another fairly often, in case we should be suddenly taken away to be tried.

Since what Richard told me was under the seal of the confessional, I could not reveal it. I could only try to dissuade him from his purpose. When that failed, I begged him to tell Christopher as well.

"Why, Paul, he's the last person! A so-called Catholic, who

wants to be friends with the Government! I wouldn't think of telling him."

As a last resort, I refused Richard absolution. He burst into tears. "Why, Paul, I thought you were so clear, so firm. Now you're talking as if you believed what Christopher said. But you'll never change me, Paul. If prison can shake and weaken even a man like you — well, that only makes me all the more determined."

I rose up the next day heavy with Richard's confession. Heavy still, that afternoon, I stood in Christopher's room, talking of the latest news — that the Jesuit Father Weston, my superior (though I had never seen him) was taken. He had been found in Arundel Castle, and because of this the Earl of Arundel was now in the Tower.

As we talked, we looked out at the river. A barge was coming towards us, a nobleman's barge, richly painted and gilded, with a coat of arms on its prow.

Our warders came bustling in; they too had seen this barge. It did not belong to any of the great men from the court. But, to be on the safe side, they bundled us into our separate rooms.

I was glad to be alone. Every moment I spent with Christopher increased my temptation to tell him more than I should. Why did I feel so strong an impulse to consult him? I did not, after all, believe half he told me.

Outside, I heard the warders making their usual parade for a visiting nobleman. I heard them say: "My lord . . ." And he corrected them. "No, I'm not a lord. Call me Mr. Cotton."

I was in my right mind, neither fasting nor dreaming. Yet surely I knew that voice.

The warder noisily unlocked my door. A graceful young man, ruffed and curled and adorned with embroidery, stood on my threshold. He told the warder to wait outside, and gave him a whole silver shilling. Only when the grateful man had locked us in together did we clasp hands.

"Robert!" I whispered. "Robert Southwell!"

"You have to call me Mr. Cotton, secretary to the Countess of Arundel."

"Is that a safe thing to be? I heard the Earl of Arundel was in the Tower."

"That makes it all the safer. The Countess, you see, has come to court to plead for him. So she has a good reason for living in her London house. And for having a secretary to look after her legal business. What's more, everyone thinks that she doesn't agree with her husband. He scarcely spoke to her for years, until Father Weston reconciled him to the Church. Then it turned out that *she* had been reconciled to the Church, unbeknown to her husband, by another priest. So Father Weston brought husband and wife together."

"Thank God for that, at least!" I said. Robert looked surprised. I told him that some Catholics complained of Jesuit influence on their wives.

"Yes, English Catholics are very confused, aren't they? The women are to blame, if you get to the bottom of it. I'm writing a poem about that; would you like to see it?"

"Very much."

"It's only a fragment so far." He read aloud:

"O women, woe to men: traps for their falls,
Still actors in all tragical mischances:
Earth's necessary evils, captiving thralls,
Now murdering with your tongues, now with your glances,
Parents of life and love: spoilers of both,
The thieves of hearts: false do you love or loathe."

I said: "Perhaps you shouldn't show that to the Countess of Arundel."

"Oh, she wouldn't be interested; she's busy with her new baby. She keeps it in her private apartments, thank goodness; I live on the other side of the house. It's very convenient. I have everything I could want there—even a printing press."

"So you can print your poems."

"I can print what's much more urgently needed—the clear teaching of the Church. It's time to put a stop to these complaints and brabblings among our own people. By the grace of God, Father Garnett and I have arrived here at the right moment."

"Father Garnett? Our old lecturer?"

"Yes; he travelled with me. Father Parsons came to see us off on the Ponte Milvio. He said we were two arrows aiming at one target."

"Father Parsons made a parade of seeing you off? On the Milvio Bridge? In broad daylight?"

"Why not?"

"Were you in disguise?"

"No; we travelled as Jesuits, staying at religious houses, all the way to Rouen."

"Had you quarrelled with Father Parsons? Was there something against you?"

"Why, Paul, what do you mean?"

I remembered then what Father Parsons had against him. I put my head into my hands and groaned.

"Paul! What's the matter?"

"Don't think I blame you, Robert; we can't help our thoughts. And we mustn't conceal them from a superior. Not even our most private feelings. But something you said . . . I expect it was misunderstood . . . The story followed me here. Walsingham called me a sodomite."

"That can't have been from anything I said."

"Then was Parsons telling me lies?"

"Father Parsons would never tell you a lie, Paul. You mustn't think that. Perhaps I was mistaken. Let me see . . . Father Parsons did ask me whether I thought you were beautiful. I said yes."

"Oh God."

"Well, I can't help that, Paul. You are beautiful."

"Did you say any more than that?"

"Well, yes. I had to. He asked me—was your beauty the sort of beauty that aroused my desire? I said I had sometimes been aware of that. I said I had examined my conscience about it. But then I decided that the main reason why I took so much delight in your face was that it put me in mind of spiritual beauty. It made me pray for you to be as radiant in your soul. I was in the middle of explaining that to Father Parsons when he dismissed me. Perhaps he was too busy to follow exactly what I said."

"You must have had other conversations with Parsons."

"He prepared me, of course, before I left Rome. He asked me whether I meant to speak against the Government or the Queen. I said no. He said that was right."

"What did Father Garnett say about that?"

"The same, I think. But of course I wasn't there when Father Parsons prepared him."

"Robert, please tell me again about your journey. You left Rome undisguised. You came to Rouen undisguised. What happened then?"

"The Jesuit Fathers in Rouen dressed us as travelling horse dealers. At least, that's what they said. I don't think the clothes were quite right. I haven't seen anything like them since I've been in England. But, as it turned out, nobody ever saw them. We were supposed to land at Newhaven, but the ship was blown off course. We went aground on a beach in the moonlight. The captain shouted for help, and some fishermen came with lanterns. From what they said I understood we were near Arundel. So, while the fishermen were wading round the ship on one side, Father Garnett and I slid on ropes down the other side, and found our way along the river by moonlight to Arundel Castle. We knew the Earl was a Catholic, but we had no idea that he was hiding our superior in England, Father Weston."

"Then this was before Father Weston was taken."

"Two days before. We only had that little time with him. He was very much concerned about you, Paul. He wanted to know if they'd asked you the Bloody Question."

"You mean — where I landed?"

"No, I suppose they have a right to ask you that. English law's concerned with facts, and that's a fact — you did land. But to ask what you *would* do in a hypothetical case — that's not according to law. Walsingham actually asks our people what side they would be on, if the Spaniards landed."

"Oh yes, he asked me."

"And what did you say?"

"That I'd be on the side of my country and my Queen."

Robert looked at me dubiously. "I suppose it's all right to say that . . . As it's not a question of the Faith. Only . . . did he believe you?"

"No. He said in that case I couldn't be a Catholic. I told him that one Catholic prince or another is always fighting the Pope."

"Paul! You shouldn't have said that."

"Why not? He must know it already."

"But when we're talking to our enemies, we have to make a point of our unity. We belong to one Church, which always teaches the same thing. Not like the heretics, fighting among themselves — Lutherans against Calvinists, Puritans against the so-called Church of England."

"But we do fight among ourselves."

"It's all very well to be truthful, Paul, but you know what they taught us at college. We are not bound to answer every question put to us by everybody."

"I didn't answer the questions about where I landed."

"Oh, good. You protected the Catholics who helped you."

"As a matter of fact, the people who helped me were Puritans."

"Then why protect them? I can't understand it, Paul. It must be the English weather. Nobody here has any *clarity*. There's a mist round the edges of good and evil."

"There's a mist in my mind, certainly. Look, Robert. You landed safely — because you were off course. Your clothes were good enough — because nobody saw them. Now, did you have any evidence afterwards that the Queen's men were expecting you?"

"Of course they were. They came from Newhaven — "

"The place where you should have landed?"

"Yes. They came to Arundel Castle because it's known as a

Catholic house. They were asking for us by name. Father Garnett and I could hear every word they said. There wasn't even a proper wall between us — only a partition. But they never found our hiding-place. The sad thing was, they found the other one, where Father Weston was. And then they found the Earl and Countess had slipped away. They were already on a ship, going overseas. A coastguard ship overtook it, and arrested the Earl."

"Will they torture the Earl," I asked, "to make him say where you are?"

"Torture a nobleman! Don't be ridiculous, Paul! No, the Earl's being very well treated. Sad, of course, that the search wasn't twenty-four hours later. Then he and the Countess would have been safe with the Prince of Parma."

"The Prince of —"

"Ssh! Don't shout! The Earl had a letter to give him. Thank God, he threw it overboard, while the coastguards were boarding the ship. It was from the Queen of Scots, you see. The Prince of Parma wants to marry her."

I felt myself about to faint. Robert put a kind, sustaining arm about me.

"Never mind, Paul. I'm sure the Queen of Scots will find someone else to carry her letter."

"She will!" I groaned. "I know she will."

Shaking from head to foot, I found my duplicate key, and opened the door. I led Robert towards Richard Sherwood's room. A warder intercepted us.

"Don't, sir!" he whispered in my ear. "For the love of God, don't lead the gentleman this way!"

I said: "He's not from the court; he can't bring trouble on you." Then I took in the full meaning of the warder's entreaty. I said: "Has Father Sherwood run away?"

The warder made as if to put a finger over my mouth. But the finger trembled, uncertain, in mid-air. "Slipped out, sir, slipped out, as any of you might. To the pie-shop round the corner, I dare say. When the main gate's open, to let in the brewer's dray, what's to stop anyone? But it's awkward, sir, his not being there if we have an inspection."

I whispered to Robert: "There'll be trouble over this. You'd better go while you can."

He took his leave without apparent haste. "Father Garnett is our superior now," he murmured into my ear. "Consult him before you do anything."

"But where can I find him?"

"You can't. He'll find you."

Then Robert resumed his nobleman's airs, calling to his boatmen as languidly as if he were on his way from one idle pleasure to the next.

I went immediately to Christopher and said: "Richard Sherwood has run away."

"How do you know?" he asked me. Then, looking into my face: "You knew beforehand!"

"Yes, he told me, but under—"

"—the seal of the Confessional! Paul, you fool! How could you let him tie your hands like that? Why didn't you make your confession to me? Then *I* would have known it under the seal of the Confessional. I couldn't have told anyone else about it, but at least we could have discussed it between us."

"I never thought of that."

"Well, confess to me now. And don't go on about the usual things. Your lustful feelings for your female penitents . . .Your pride . . . What I want to know is how bad things are."

They were, we agreed, bad enough. By escaping, Richard had broken our unwritten pact with the Government. We could no longer expect to enjoy the same liberty. But the worst thing was his reason for escaping. It seemed to Christopher and me, as we talked over Robert Southwell's account, that pure chance—in the shape of over-zealous local searchers—had prevented the Earl of Arundel from taking the Scottish Queen's letter to the Prince of Parma. Walsingham had surely meant him to take it. Now he had to find another messenger. It could not be coincidence that, a few days after the Earl's arrest, an unknown 'good Catholic' had approached Richard

Sherwood, offering to smuggle him aboard a ship in the Pool of London — an impossible thing to arrange, as we knew, without Walsingham's connivance. All Richard had to do in return was carry some letters from the Queen of Scots.

"How could you let him go?" asked Christopher.

"I did my best," I said. "I refused him absolution. If he dies now . . ."

"He's not likely to die just yet. Walsingham intends him to get safe across."

"Not to be captured with the letters on him?"

"What for? Walsingham already has copies. We can be sure of that. No; he wants to see how far the Queen of Scots will go."

"But how can she be such a fool?"

"You can't know much about her previous life. That letter Walsingham read you, Paul — you thought it was preposterous. It would be, if addressed to a reasonable person. But it was a good letter to send the Queen of Scots. Father Parsons did his work well."

"No! It wasn't Father Parsons' letter. It was a forgery by Walsingham."

Christopher looked at me.

"All right, then!" I said. "I'll escape myself."

"What for? To warn the Queen of Scots that her letters are intercepted? If she's determined to lay her own head on the block, neither you nor I can stop her."

"It's not that. I have to go back to Rome and . . . ask some questions. Because I can't bear what you say about Father Parsons. I can't bear to hear these . . . these bits of gossip from here and there, all pointing to a conclusion which . . . which can't be true! Which mustn't be true! I can't go on living in that state of mind."

IX

I HAD TO GO ON LIVING, not in that state, but in a worse
one. When Richard's escape was known, we were locked up in
earnest. No visitors were admitted. No food might be sent in.
Instead of the pleasant meals we had enjoyed in common, we
took the messes from the prison kitchen, which the warders
brought slowly, half cold, to each room.

The Clink is not so strongly built as the Tower, and there
are some rotten places in the walls. "A chink in the Clink!"
said my nearest neighbour, John Mush, when we found that
we could converse through such a hole. He was in high spirits.
Now that prison had brought him real privations, he was less
tormented by the memory of Margaret Clitheroe.

I, on the contrary, was more tormented. Each fragment of
news increased my misery.

From the gossip that seeped through the 'chinks in the
Clink', we guessed that something more than Richard's
escape had caused this change in our treatment. But it was
from a warder that I first heard the name *Babington*.

A young Catholic gentleman, Anthony Babington, with his

friends, had formed a plot to murder the Queen. The warder said that a priest called Ballard had encouraged them. I said: "I don't believe that!" but I said it after a pause. A few days later I heard that the Queen of Scots had written a letter wishing Anthony Babington well. To this news I said nothing.

I could not speak directly to Christopher. He was on the other side of the building. In my mind I argued with him passionately. "You say that Father Parsons intended you and me to be caught. And Robert Southwell? Why Robert Southwell? Just for saying I was beautiful? And Father Garnett? What could he have against Father Garnett?"

As if Christopher were in the room with me, I was aware of the answer. In his lectures, Father Garnett had often said: "Of course, England is ruled by law." He would not want it to be ruled by Spanish courts-martial.

I checked myself. It was more rational to suppose that Parsons and Englefield had abandoned the plan of disguising people before they left Rome. There was no purpose in it, since Walsingham's men would in any case report on them when they were seen at Rouen.

But then, why go on sending them by Rouen? If they were not meant to be caught . . . If they were not supposed to be found plotting with the Queen of Scots . . .

This was madness. Had I stood firm under interrogation, firm under torture, to let my faith crumble now?

Oh Lord God, since I am so feeble, since the knowledge of Thy grace is not company enough, send me one human being I can trust!

That prayer at least was answered. One morning, when I called John Mush through the hole in the wall, he shushed me. "I'm busy, Paul." I went away from the hole and waited a while, then returned. It seemed to me I could hear whispering. Were there two voices in the room? John raised his voice, to say: "*Ego te absolvo.*" And I heard the rustle of a woman's dress, as the penitent rose from her knees.

"John!" I called. "Are they letting us hear confessions again?"

"Only this one," he replied. "They won't let in anybody but Anne Clitheroe."

I cried out: "Oh, let me see her too!"

Anne's voice replied: "Yes, Father Calverley, I am coming to see you!"

Soon she appeared, with a warder, who said that he must be present while we talked. Anne had brought me a pork pie and a bottle of wine. Hungry as I was, I scarcely looked at these things. I could not take my eyes off her face. I knew now why it had seemed familiar from the first. It was the face of the vision I hoped one day to have; the face that would advance to meet me, smiling, across flowers uncrushed by human feet.

Yet this was a real girl; she could not have hovered or floated into my prison. "How did they come to let you in?" I asked.

She said: "I suppose they grew tired of keeping me out."

The warder laughed. "Easier to keep out the birds of Heaven."

Then he bowed to Anne, as if sorry for his presumption, and stood back as far as he could, while we talked.

"Here's a letter from your father and mother," she said. "They're well . . . And what a blessing it was that they left London when they did! All the Catholics in London feel themselves in danger. Nobody can tell who's going to be arrested next, for this pretended plot."

"Are you sure it's only pretended?" I asked her.

"Well . . . Father Mush told me I shouldn't be so quick to draw conclusions. But what Catholic would really try to kill the Queen, knowing the misfortune he'd be bringing on the heads of other Catholics? And how could the Queen of Scots be such a fool — ?"

The warder shifted his feet, and coughed.

"We know nothing about these matters," I said. "Is there any news affecting us directly?"

"Yes, I'm afraid there is. All of you in the Clink are going to be sent to Wisbech Castle."

"God forbid!"

"At least that means they're not putting you on trial. Or . . . or anything worse. Wisbech isn't a bad place. And it's northwards—north of Cambridge. Almost half way to York. You'll be a hundred miles nearer your father and mother."

I thought for a moment, then asked her: "Do you know enough Latin to say your prayers?"

"More than that! I used to help my brothers with their lessons."

"Say some Latin to me."

She began: "*Arma virumque cano* . . ."

I smiled at seeing her so proud of her learning, which indeed was unusual in a butcher's daughter. After a dozen lines I stopped her, and intoned in Latin, as if it were a prayer: "I must escape, and soon, before they shut me into that castle."

She intoned her answer, as if making the responses to a prayer.

"Tell me, Father, what I am to do."

"Buy a good horse. When we are taken to that place, see that some Catholic ladies, yourself among them, ride after us, keeping as near as the guards will allow. Be always near me, Anne; be always ready to give up your horse to me."

"Father, I shall do as you say."

The warder told us that Anne had outstayed her time.

She cried out: "But I want to see the other priests! I have a pie and a flask for each one."

"I'll take those to the gentlemen," said the warder.

She thanked him, and held out his usual fee. He amazed us both by refusing. "If you'll just say a prayer for me, Miss, in your Latin . . . They can say what they like, but that Latin's a blessed language! You can't tell me that a prayer in English does the same good."

When I was alone again, I heard the voice of John Mush. "Paul, you swine!" Then he went into Italian, for fear we were overheard. He showered me with reproaches, asking finally: "What do you think you're doing to Anne?"

"She's willing to help me."

"Willing! She's delighted! And you trade on that. You ask her to die for you."

"I didn't mean that."

"What else did you mean?"

"I'd make it look as if I'd stolen the horse from her."

"And Walsingham would be completely taken in! You think so? When you're captured — as you will be, after half-an-hour — they'll open the saddle bags and find the provisions Anne has put there for you. And they'll find a complete set of men's clothes — she'll have made that ready to the last stitch, knowing her. Then they'll believe that Anne just happened to have those things in her saddle bags, when you stole her horse."

"Why should I be captured in half-an-hour?"

"Because you'll be riding round in circles. You don't know the way to anywhere."

"That's not true. I know the road to Colchester. And beyond there I know a place where I think I can get out of the country."

"I bet Walsingham knows it better than you."

"No. That was what they were trying to rack out of me."

"Are you sure you said nothing on the rack?"

"Yes; I was lucky; I fainted."

He sighed so loud, I could hear him through the wall. "You're a good boy, Paul, in your way. But thoughtless! Even if you remember the road from London to Colchester, how can you find it from the other road — the road we're taking?"

"The road to Colchester runs north-east. If they're going to take us northwards, I'll have to turn right at the first opportunity."

"Suppose your first opportunity came at Ware. You can hardly count on a break in the journey sooner than that. And until there is a break you'll be on some bony old mare, your feet tied under its belly and your hands bound, so that you have no control of stirrup or reins. You have to go where the guard leads you. That's how they brought me here, and, believe me, Paul, it's a wretched way to ride. You'll be worn out and covered with bruises by the time you reach Ware. Well, then suppose they untie you—let you go to the privy, have something to eat at the inn . . . That's your moment, eh? You take poor Anne's horse, and you turn right. Well, yes; that would bring you to Colchester, after about fifty miles, if you knew the way. But you don't know the way, Paul, and you daren't ask. And the horse isn't fresh. No more are you. You can't ride fifty miles in a night."

"I'd spend the night in a wood."

"In this weather? We're in England, Paul; the autumn's cold and wet. And the saddle? What will you do for a saddle? You can't use Anne's. Of course, you're a good boy; you never look at a woman. If you did look at one, you'd see she was riding side-saddle."

"I could ride bare-back for a while. I used to do that as a boy."

"You're mad! I won't let you embroil that girl in your madness. Anne may think the sun shines out of your eyes. But I'm her confessor; I can tell her—no!"

We heard the warder's footsteps, and fell silent. I was now tormented with remorse. In asking Anne's help I had acted as no Jesuit should act—upon the impulse of the moment. I had not weighed the danger I was bringing her. The roughest men, in that girl's presence, were abashed. Simple people, forbidden to pay their ancient homage to saints, paid homage to Anne. I alone was treating her as a means to an end. My desire to escape had so possessed me that I no longer thought of human creatures, except as they hindered, or might help, my plan. While I was meditating on my selfish nature, I discovered that I had already eaten Anne's pork pie, and drunk her wine.

That evening John Mush called me to the wall again. He said in Italian: "I've been consulting Christopher—at second hand, you know. Through the wall the other side of me, along the rain gutters, and so on. He says you have such good reason for escaping that perhaps we ought to help you."

"Then Christopher approves!"

"Not yet. He said—not unless you were calm and collected."

"How can I be calm until I do escape? What you say about Father Parsons . . . How can you be content merely to say it? Either it's true, and he should be confronted with it. Or it's not true, and he should be warned that by some . . . carelessness he's laid himself open to these terrible slanders."

"He'll forgive you for calling him a villain, rather than calling him careless. Woe betide anyone who suggests to old Parsons that he isn't the world's most expert conspirator."

"John, I can't listen any more to what you say about him. I can't! I have to see him face to face."

"Well! It's time someone did, and it had better be a Jesuit. The trouble is, Paul, if you do escape, I'll have to escape with you."

"Why?"

"Because I know my way about England. I'm the only person in the Clink who does. The rest were captured almost as they landed. I've had three years of riding from house to house, from hide to hide. Oh, it can be done! Only, after they killed Margaret Clitheroe, I lost heart. I stopped caring for my own life. That's how I came to be taken. Perhaps if I had your life to care for as well as my own . . . But we'll have to make a reasonable plan."

Since Anne was the only person allowed to visit us, she had after all to be part of the plan. John Mush intoned his instructions to her in stately Latin, sinking his voice to a whisper whenever he came to the name of a place or a person.

"God forgive us both!" John said to me afterwards. "Do you know how old that girl is? Eighteen."

Anne did not come to see us for three days before we left. As we had foreseen, we prisoners were followed out of London by a crowd of pious Catholics. John Mush called loudly to some of those in the crowd: "Is Anne Clitheroe here?" They answered no; she had gone back to her father in York.

I began to sing. I had not been able to make music in my cage. But now, though I was bound, I had free air in my lungs, free people in my sight. I sang in English, and the English crowd did not, like the Italians, listen and admire. They joined in. Even the guards began to hum in tune with our old Catholic songs.

At first these guards were watchful. But our prisoner's way of riding, painful for us, was almost as bad for them. To ride one horse and lead another by the reins is never easy, and it must be harder when the horse that you are leading carries a dead weight, in the shape of a man who cannot control it. By afternoon our guards were quietly loosening our bonds, letting us put our feet in the stirrups and our hands to the reins. They were comforted to see that we made no attempt to escape — not even when we stopped for the night at Ware.

Indeed I could not have escaped on that first night. After seven months in prison, the exercise, the freshness of the autumn air, were utterly exhausting. The very colours of the leaves wore out my eyes. On the faces of my companions I saw the same weariness. Though it was a great pleasure to be having supper with them again, to see Christopher smile across the table at me, I could not say much, that first evening. I dropped asleep among my guards, almost before I had finished saying my prayers.

But the next morning, riding north, I sang again. Our pious followers were fewer now, but the cottagers came out to look at us, and listen. We were all wearing our priestly garments, because we wanted to show the people that we were priests, not traitors. There were some who shook their fists at us; this was a Protestant part of England. But some kneeled, asking our blessing, and many joined in our songs.

My singing was interrupted, and finally brought to an end, by Christopher's noisy complaints. He was insisting that his horse was lame. The guards maintained that it was walking on four legs like any other horse. Christopher, in his most haughty drawl, told them that he had been riding before they were born. He could feel when a horse was beginning to go lame. He went slower and slower, not wanting, he said, to tire out the poor creature. At a little place called Buntingford the guards finally let him dismount, so that they could consult a blacksmith. The blacksmith said there was a nail which had worked a bit loose.

Was the horse going much farther? "To Cambridge, by nightfall," said our guards.

"Ah! Then I'll have to put you on new shoes."

The guards muttered that a village blacksmith, wanting work, had never yet been known to say that a horse's old shoes would do.

But, as Christopher was willing to pay for the new shoes, they were put on. Meanwhile the rest of us inspected our horses for loose nails, saddle sores and early symptoms of the farcy and the glanders. As they were all old, overdriven mares, we found many defects in them. The consequent arguments with our guards lasted over two hours. By the time we were on the road again, it was too late to reach Cambridge by nightfall. We had to stop at Royston, which is not so much a town as a place where six roads meet.

"Thank God!" muttered John Mush as we dismounted. "I remembered this right. The place has only one inn."

Christopher was saying to our guards: "At least let's take these poor beasts to the stable. They might go better tomorrow if we made sure that the inn servants rubbed them down and fed them properly."

"Yes, and while we're about it," put in John Mush, "we can see that your horses are properly stabled as well."

This pleased our guards. It was a cold October evening, and they were clearly longing to be inside the inn. They left only one of their number to watch us while we stabled the horses.

Christopher once more began to find fault with everything, very noisily, in the middle of the stable yard. The inn servants gathered round him, assuring him that the stables were not so tumbledown as they looked. Nor was the hay really mouldy.

From the door of an outhouse came a groom I did not know. He murmured: "This way, sir." I followed him, and John Mush followed me.

Inside the outhouse two horses were saddled and ready. The groom gave us each a long cloak and a hat.

"The hats won't fit you very well," whispered Anne's voice

out of the darkness. "I couldn't measure you, with the warder looking on."

"They'll do," I whispered back.

John Mush was ready first.

"Pray for me!" she said as he mounted.

"And you for me!" he answered.

She said: "It's the road where the signpost says Duxford, and then the fourth lane to the right."

As I was groping for my horse, Anne threw her arms about my neck, and kissed me on the mouth. In an instant she had let me go again, and the groom was helping me into the saddle.

We rode quietly round to the front of the inn — two gentlemen on good horses, in fine feathered hats, the rest of our clothes concealed under cloaks — and were gone. We did not begin to gallop until we were out of sight of the inn. Soon the night put us out of sight of everyone. There was just enough moonlight for us to tell road from ditch.

After some five miles John caught my rein. "There's the fourth turning!" he said. We went right, into a lane so muddy that it slowed us down. And now on the wind I caught the sound of horses following ours.

"Not such good horses, though," John said. "Nor so fresh."

We plunged on, through the mud. Once more I heard the other horses. Fresh or not, they seemed to be keeping up a good pace. John dismounted, and led his horse through a gate into a field. I followed. We both stood still in the field, listening. Soon we could hear halloos and cries as well as hoof-beats. But they came no nearer. Indeed, they grew fainter, and finally died away.

"They're keeping to the road," John said. "They think we went to Sawston Hall."

We resumed our wet and sticky ride along the lane. After long flounderings, we crossed a firmer road, went over a bridge, and saw against the stars the shape of a black spire.

"Saffron Walden!" John whispered. "We have to take the lane that skirts it to the north."

After that he led me along paths which would have been

puzzling by daylight. Our whole ride, I suppose, was not fifteen miles, but I was very weary of mud and water by the time we came to the gate of a large house.

We did not knock. The gate swung open at our approach, and shut again behind us, without a word. As we dismounted, the gate-keeper took our horses. A lantern came swinging towards us, carried, I thought, by a servant. But the worn face in the lantern's light had a halo of lace and muslin. Clearly, this was the mistress of the house.

In utter silence, we followed her into a firelit parlour. Here she fell on her knees and asked our blessing.

Then she rose and said, like any other lady to her guests: "My husband will be very sorry he missed you. He's away drilling the trained bands."

This excellent lady had a table ready for our supper, with wine, ham and game pies.

"There is time to eat," she said, "before I have to hide you."

"Our eating does not matter, Mrs. Wiseman," John assured her. (How could he say that? He must be as ravenous as I was.) "The question is — will the horses have time to cool down?"

"It should be two hours at least," she said. "They are bound to search my brother's house first."

John said: "Yes, we heard them taking that road."

"Good. My brother knows what to do. The searchers will have great difficulty in rousing the porter to open the gate. A quarter of an hour can be lost there."

"But even then," John said, "if they go straight into the stables and feel the horses, and find that none of them are heated by hard riding, they will know at once we are not there."

"Yet I think they will stay and search the house. Those two hiding-places that they have never been able to find are a sore point with our local men. And even if they come straight here, it is twelve miles. Oh, I think by then your horses will be as cool as the rest."

"But these local men may know the horses are not yours."

"They are ours," Mrs. Wiseman said. "That was where I took the liberty of altering your design. When Anne Clitheroe came to me, I told her that you had better use our horses. One of our grooms took them over to Royston yesterday, on the pretext of consulting a horse-doctor. So, when the men search our stables, they will find no horses except our horses, branded with our mark."

"But they will find them all — none missing. Your groom at Royston, I suppose, has reported that we stole two horses. If the same two are here — "

"In stables as large as ours, what's two more or less? Nobody knows exactly how many we own. And, if they do suspect us, that will take their minds off Anne. They will never be able to prove anything against her."

"Thank God for that!" I said. I looked with admiration at the plump, serene lady. "Was it your groom who spoke to me at the inn?"

"Yes."

"How did he know me?"

The lady smiled. "Anne Clitheroe told him to speak to the one who looked more like an angel than a man."

John laughed and told me not to blush. "Such things have been said of you before."

"If they have," I said, "they've brought me trouble."

Trouble is a weak word. Later, when I was lying on a narrow mattress, in a hole I had entered by a false fireplace, when I heard the Queen's men raging through the house, I knew that what raged within me was far more terrible.

I was twenty-five years old, and until that hour I had not known I was a man.

I had as a novice come to know the temptations of lust, and the spiritual disciplines by which our mentors taught us to overcome it. But I had never been prepared for this. To see a woman suddenly, not as a means to an end, but as a human creature, to know that this creature loved me — this was a feeling which more engrossed my soul than any feeling I had ever had for God. I wanted to protect Anne, to feel her protecting me. I wanted all my work to be for her, and all my singing. Would I grumble and quarrel, as other married men do?

Perhaps; men quarrel even with God. But I felt that the roughest labourer, who beats his wife and makes it up with her by morning, knew more of the life of the spirit than I did.

The searchers were tapping the walls, listening for a hollow sound. When they came near the hollow I was in, I did as Mrs. Wiseman had instructed me. I rolled over on the mattress and pressed my body against the wall, so that it would sound solid under the tapping. There was only the thickness of half a brick between us; the tapping made my body shake. I could hardly believe they did not hear that.

Pride kept me still and silent through the danger. Pride, I now saw, had made me a priest. I had intended to rival the saints in their glory. I had pursued their visions, by spiritual exercises, by prayers, by fasting; and had never once attained the illumination which came to me now through a young girl's kiss on my mouth.

The searchers had ceased their tapping and were calling out: "We know you're there, John Mush—old Father Mush! We know you're there, Paul Calverley, you Jesuit, you priest!"

Within myself I answered: I am Paul Calverley, but I know now that I ought not to be a Jesuit. I ought not to be a priest.

X

SINCE THE SEARCHERS WERE coming every day to count the horses in Mrs. Wiseman's stable, John and I dressed as cattle drovers, and left the house on foot. "A fine time of year you chose!" John muttered, as we splashed all night through a cold rain. In fact it was a fine time for us; our pursuers were staying indoors. Besides, the cold kept us awake and moving. We covered some twenty miles, and, well before dawn, John was making a known signal at the gate of White Notley Hall, near Witham.

Here our host was Lord Vaux of Harrowden, a man of such importance that the Queen's men always gave him fair warning before they searched his house. "That class of person," he said, "knows better than to tell me what I ought to believe."

We were only a day's ride from St. Osyth. Lord Vaux advised me to go there openly. If anybody questioned me I should say that I was going to visit Lord Darcy, who was then in residence. He was known to be a zealous Protestant. About a mile from St. Osyth Priory (Lord Darcy's house kept that name still) there was a turning where I could pretend to miss my way, and go to the tide-mill instead. I was now letting my beard grow again, because the proclamation out for me described me as clean-shaven. But the best of all disguises was, as always, to look like a gentleman. Lord Vaux called in his own tailor, a Catholic, to make new clothes for John and myself. Not until years later did I learn that he had paid the tailor by pawning his peer's robes.

Before I could set out I must, of course, confess and receive the Sacrament. I dreaded this, because it meant confessing to John.

I began well enough. "I believe," I said, "that it is my duty to make this journey. And yet I am almost prevented by fear."

"Of capture?"

"I may avoid capture. I cannot avoid being seasick."

John said that was hardly a sin. "Come, what's really on your mind?"

I hesitated.

"Lust?" he prompted.

"I don't think so."

"Envy?"

"Yes. I envy you, for being Anne Clitheroe's confessor."

He sighed. "Why won't you admit that what you feel is lust?"

"I don't think it is. What haunts me is her face. It's with me always; I live by its brightness, as I ought to live by the love of God. If I could be honourably released from my vows, then I would marry Anne. If she would have me."

"Paul! How can you talk such wicked nonsense? You can't be released from your vows. You were of age when you took them."

"Come to think of it . . . I wasn't twenty-four, the age for becoming a priest. The College arranged for us to take our vows at twenty-three, in case we should be suddenly called abroad."

"I suppose the College had a proper dispensation to do that."

"And as for being a Jesuit . . . I haven't taken final vows yet.

We are supposed to be able to change our minds, at any age up to thirty."

"These are quibbles, Paul."

"I know . . . The real thing is, it's blasphemous for me to remain a priest, when I feel I have no vocation."

"Your feelings won't interest the Pope. I suppose you think you're going to the right place. Rome can do anything . . . But that's one thing it won't do—release you from a vow of celibacy."

"In Queen Mary's time, Cardinal Pole gave dispensations like that."

"Only in special cases. There were some priests who'd been married in Protestant times. Cardinal Pole gave them leave to keep their wives, and live as Catholic laymen."

"That's all I want to do."

"But it's impossible, Paul! And in any case it's not for you. You're a lad with brains; you need companions you can talk to."

"I'd have Anne."

"Oh, nonsense! What do you know about her, after all?"

"I've seen how brave she is. I know how she went into the prisons, among murderers and thieves."

"That's easy for a girl who's young, and can't imagine real danger. It's not so tedious as doing women's work at home. She has a pretty face; you think she must have pretty brains. And what does she know about you? Did you tell her why you were going to Rome?"

"No. I can't explain all that to a lay person."

"You see? You're a priest, after all; there's a gulf dividing you from the laity. Especially from Anne. You're in a dream, Paul! A dream! And mind! Whatever else you do, don't mention this to Parsons. The lusts of the flesh put him into such a lather—"

"Please . . . Please don't say any more about Father Parsons."

"Very well. Only—remember what I have said."

What I remembered better was what he had not said. As I

128

rode through Colchester, and then along the yellowing lanes, I could think only of that. John was bound to be silent over anything Anne had confessed. But he could have told me: "Put it out of your mind! Even if you were free, she would never consent to marry you." He had not.

I might never see Anne again. I might not reach Rome alive, and how to return I could scarcely imagine. As for a dispensation from my vows, I did not know how to begin to ask.

I was aware of all this; yet I did not feel it. I did not feel the cold wind blowing off the sea. Anne loved me.

All that sweet, solitary day I rode unchallenged. At sunset I came to St. Osyth Creek. There were two or three fishing boats lying half keeled over in the mud. The tide, then, was out; the miller probably asleep. Yet I dared not wait where some passing farmer might see me. I knocked at the door of the mill.

It was opened by a sullen young man — the Puritan son? Feeling danger, I nevertheless asked to see the miller alone. He came down blinking, half asleep.

"I have five shillings to return to you," I said. "You lent it to a friend of mine. And here's another five shillings for the clothes you gave him, when he had nothing but a shirt."

The miller was wide awake when he took the money. "I suppose," he said, "after all the trouble you had landing here you want to be away again . . . Are you the fellow they put on the rack?"

"Yes. They wanted to know where I'd landed, and whose house I'd sheltered in."

"And you never told 'em?"

"You know I didn't. You'd be in prison if I had."

"Ah! And so I might be, if I help you now."

"Yes, that's true. I can pay you danger money . . ."

He said nothing.

"Well!" I said. "If you can't help me, tell me so at once, and I'll go back to wait . . . where I have been waiting."

"What, with old Foxy, at White Notley Hall? I heard there was a couple of priests lying low there."

"Where did you hear that?"

"Why, from everybody. All of us in these parts know when old Foxy's hiding a priest. That's th'only time he do ever spend any money. That horse'll be his, ah? My son can ride that back to White Notley Hall tomorrow, and then see a friend of ours about a boat for you."

He called his son to put the horse in a shed for the night. Then he showed me the hayloft where I was to sleep. "I suppose you'd rather have hay in your clothes than flour dust? Easier to beat out."

When I sat down to share their bread and cheese, the son glanced at me sidelong, under black brows. I said: "You came back safe, then, from the Low Countries?"

He looked away, and growled.

"Now, Nick!" said his father. "Won't hurt 'ee to be civil. The gentleman meant no harm. He's not to know you deserted."

"I didn't desert," the lad muttered.

"Whatever you did," I told him, "it's no business of mine." As I said this I knew I did not feel it. In that way I would always be a priest; it was my business what other people did.

"Nothing to be so snarky over," Nick's father told him. "First time in your life you showed a bit of sense. If she up the road don't like it, more fool her."

"Give over, will you?" Nick shouted.

I said: "You should not raise your voice to your father."

He muttered: "Raise my hand to him, if he won't give over." Then, mastering himself: "You don't know, sir, what I've put up with, since I came back. The Brethren call me a deserter, and . . . and there's some won't speak to me."

"There's one young woman won't," his father corrected. "Women! They love a soldier. Let him show plenty of scars, they never ask — was it in a just cause?"

I said: "Then you believe now it wasn't a just cause?"

Nick declared: "The cause was right! And still is. I still say we'll have to fight the Spaniards for our freedom, and better now than later. The trouble, sir, is all in our own army.

Sweepings, broken men! The minute the Earl of Leicester took his eye off 'em, they were behaving like Spaniards. Looting the liquor, attacking the women . . . Every night in camp I used to reason with 'em—them as were sober enough to be reasoned with. I'd say: 'Have you forgotten you have immortal souls?' They used to tell me to mind my own business. I said it was my business if I saw my fellow-creatures going to damnation. Well, sir, we had a bad day's fighting at a place called Zutphen. Half of us killed, and the rest could get nothing to eat. I told my companions it was God's judgment on us. That did it. They set on me and beat me senseless. The next I knew, I was lying on a Dutch barge, among the wounded. I suppose the Dutch people thought I'd been hurt in the fighting. I couldn't tell 'em no other, not knowing their lingo. The barge was going down a river. Every day some of the wounded fellows died, and the bargemen threw 'em overboard. One day I began helping to throw 'em, so I knew I was better. When we came to Amsterdam I met an English captain who wanted a deckhand. I don't know. I suppose my duty was to find my old companions, and let them beat me again. Instead I took the hand that was held out to me, and came back here. What would you have done?"

"Not gone back to the same companions. But . . . wasn't there some English officer that you might have appealed to?"

"Talk to an officer! Why, that would have been telling tales."

"I'd have told some tales, if they'd come looking for him," said the miller. "But nobody looks for deserters; there's too many."

"Don't you keep calling me a deserter!" Nick said. "To my way of thinking, the army deserted me."

The miller began to tell me how he meant to smuggle me overseas. "Lucky for you there's this army in the Low Countries. Plenty of ships going over with salt beef and bacon for 'em."

"They sell that where they do dock, then," said Nick. "We soldiers never had a smell of it."

"Ay, they'll break the laws for money," his father agreed. "That's what this gentleman is hoping for. Now! Buttermouth and Grumble are in jail. But there's a fellow used to work with 'em, till they got greedy. Master of a sloop. We'll send him word to anchor off Colne Point when he's next passing."

"A sloop?" I asked. "Isn't that a very small boat?"

"Ay. Oh, ay; you'll know you're on the waves, when you're in that."

This prospect made the miller's hayloft seem a very comfortable place. Once more I had nothing to read but Fox's *Book of Martyrs*, and the Protestant version of the Bible. But now everything I read became an occasion for an argument with young Nick. My Jesuit education stood me in good stead. I never lost my temper, nor said anything to wound his self-esteem. Gently, I pointed out the contradictions in Calvin's teaching, and Luther's.

"I don't go by Luther," he said. "Nor Calvin. I go by the Bible, and the light within me."

As he hung over a rafter, trying to mend one of the applewood teeth on the gearwheels of the mill, he explained to me this light within. It told him, for example, that smuggling was not wrong. "Only breaking man's laws, not God's."

I said: "It's to my advantage that you should think so. And yet I would rather you helped me because I am doing God's work, than because it's against the law."

He replied: "The best God's work you ever did was to break these laws against travelling. Because that's God's will — you'll never convince me other. We should come and go as we please."

Here he decided that the wheel he was tinkering with would have to be lifted out bodily. I helped him. "Mind, sir! That's heavy. All oak, apart from the teeth." He was surprised to find how strong I was in lifting, though I could not match his dexterity of hand. "You'd make a good soldier, sir!"

When we had the wheel propped up in the barn, and Nick was knocking out its broken tooth, he told me more about the light within. It had shown him he was not doing wrong, to lie in the hay with a girl he had honestly meant to marry. "When I was doing that every night, sir, I was full of good thoughts. But since my sweetheart took against me, I've turned sour as vinegar. Sometimes I want to kill the stupid slut! I can feel my fingers itching to go round her throat. And then it all comes back, how sweet she used to be. When I was going to the war, she cried, and clung to me, and kissed my mouth . . ."

I found I was listening. Not listening in order to refute his arguments, but listening in order to hear. It was a new feeling. I could no longer say: "Nevertheless, it was wrong." He had been happy then. How could he repent? Only I thought of Anne, and pitied Nick with all my soul, because the girl that he had loved was bigoted and stupid.

A fortnight after I came to the mill, Nick rowed me down the creek in the dark. I began to feel sick before we left Brightlingsea Reach. I knew that in the open sea I should be speechless, and so I hastened to thank him there and then.

"Don't you thank me, sir!" he whispered. "Too many Papists in England — only right I should make it one less!"

XI

"NOBODY CROSSES THE ALPS in winter," the Fathers told me in Rouen.

"Somebody must," I said, "or the monks of St. Bernard would be lonely."

"But it's cold. It's dangerous. Why don't you go to Marseilles, and then by sea?"

Still weak from seasickness, and bruised from being thrown against the bulkheads of the sloop, I said that I would rather face rock and avalanche. While I was disputing the point, the Jesuit House had a visitor, the Monsieur Delahaye whom they had once called in to inspect my disguise. It had been at the back of my mind that he might have given my description to Walsingham. I would rather believe that than . . . But now, seeing that he scarcely recognised me, I could not believe he had looked at me long enough to write a description.

Monsieur Delahaye told the Jesuits that his master, the Duke of Guise, was sending him with an urgent message to Rome. He would carry their letters too, if they had any signed and sealed; but he could not wait above an hour.

"Quick!" said my compatriots. "Write at once and ask Father Parsons what you are to do."

"I will ask him that in person," I said.

Monsieur Delahaye agreed to take me as interpreter, for he spoke hardly any Italian. He lent me one of the Duke's horses. Amid his numerous companions, I was the only man not armed to the teeth, for I travelled now as a priest, in my Jesuit habit.

We rode fast. The message from the Duke of Guise was an appeal for the life of his first cousin, the Queen of Scots. He was begging the Pope to intervene.

I asked M. Delahaye what made the Duke suppose that this was possible. "The Pope is not on speaking terms with Queen Elizabeth."

"Oh, he is," M. Delahaye said. "There are English envoys in Rome. They pretend to be merchants, but what they're after is to persuade the Pope that Elizabeth would grant freedom to Catholics, if the Catholics would give up their plots against her. They have enough money, these English; they've won over two or three cardinals, and what that must cost . . . Now the Pope can say to them—here's your chance! If Elizabeth is as merciful as you make out, you can persuade her to save that poor lady's life."

In the warm country south of Paris it was autumn still. We rode through villages which ought to have been busy with noises of threshing and milling. Instead the threshing-barns were burned, the people gone. Here and there some wretched creature would start up from the roadside, crying out: "We have nothing to eat but grass!" Without slackening their pace, M. Delahaye and his companions would shout back: "What do you expect, from Huguenots?" If they found that it was Catholics who had burned the district they would say: "Ah! Our boys do their work properly."

If I paused a moment, to give what little I could to the starving, my companions would shout at me. Once, when I stopped long enough to give the last rites to a dying child, these good Catholics accused me of delaying their journey. I replied: "Your journey will be under a curse." This was not well taken, since we were about to cross the Alps.

When we had climbed and plunged and slithered over to the Italian side, they wanted to celebrate their safety by going to a brothel. I told them they could not do it, if they had a right understanding of love. They retorted that I, as a priest, was no doubt an authority on love. M. Delahaye urged them along the road, and in fact they had no time for the brothel. But they still muttered at me. It was from a few words dropped on this occasion that I learned the true meaning of M. Delahaye's kind offer to carry the Jesuit's letters. The Duke of Guise wanted to read them. "Who knows what new mischief they're plotting?" I pretended not to hear this. When we reached Rome, I was glad to relinquish my horse and say farewell to them all, at the gate of the French ambassador's house.

I ran all the way to the English College. It was the beginning of December, 1586 — just over a year after I had left.

Father Agazzari greeted me with delight. "What a joy it is, Paul, when one of our boys comes back safe! Richard Sherwood is here, you know, but so ill and weak . . . And you look thin. Sit here and rest, while I send a message to Father Parsons."

I told him I could not rest. "You, Father, appointed Father Parsons my superior. I have something urgent to say, and I must say it to him alone. Please tell me where he is."

With reluctance, Father Agazzari told me that Parsons had moved into the house of Sir Francis Englefield.

When I came to that house I did not give the servants my name. I told them only to say that a man had come from England with urgent news. I was admitted at once, and saw what I had most feared to see — that both Parsons and Englefield started back.

Parsons at once recovered, and began positively to fawn on me. "Why, Paul! One of our heroes — one of our real heroes. This is a great day! We must make a feast for you. A Roman chicken . . . Wine from Frascati . . ."

I looked at Sir Francis, and saw him give Parsons an admiring smile. "Yes, indeed!" he said. "You are most welcome,

Father Calverley. I will go and give the servants orders for this feast."

Left alone with Parsons, I went down on my knees.

"Father!" I said. "You are my superior. By my vows I must obey you. It is my duty to tell you what I have heard and seen in England, holding nothing back."

"Yes, Paul, tell me everything. Don't kneel; sit here by the brazier."

Sitting beside me, he seemed so much my friend that I felt I must have misread his first emotion. I told my story calmly enough, until I came to the letter read aloud by Walsingham's secretary. There I found myself trembling.

"Father, I told Walsingham that you could not have written it."

"Good, Paul, very good. That was the right thing to say."

"I thought it was obvious. Because whoever wrote that letter wasn't giving the Queen of Scots useful advice. He was putting her head on the block."

He looked at me in a fatherly way, and said: "So that's how it seems to you, Paul, is it?"

"Well, surely . . . Urging her to escape—as if she needed urging! Taking it for granted that she approved of the plans for a Spanish invasion! And then suggesting that she should offer herself as a wife to the Prince of Parma, so as to make him even more anxious to invade . . . That letter could hardly come from a friend."

"It may interest you," said Parsons, rising, "to know that the lady herself disagrees with you. In her reply she addresses me as 'Good Friend'."

He unlocked a cabinet and brought out a letter, which he put into my hands.

The letter did indeed begin: "Good Friend". The Queen of Scots went on to say that she might have been able to escape when she was at Wingfield, if she had had enough money. But now, at Chartley, she was so closely guarded that she had not been able to win any of the household to her side, except one man who was carrying the letter.

I cried out: "If she really believes that the man who carries her letters is devoted to her, if she does not know that he's a spy for Walsingham — "

Parsons cut me short. "Really, Paul! There are people with more experience in these matters than you."

I went on reading the letter. It urged Parsons to "continue to labour by all means for the re-establishment of things in this country." Then it expressed "right affectionate thanks" to the Prince of Parma. "As it hath pleased the King of Spain . . . to make a special choice of him to have from henceforth the whole charge and managing of the enterprise proposed for the re-establishing of this state, so in as much as I can for my own part I shall always esteem it for me no small happiness to concur in an action so important . . ."

"She concurs!" I said. "And puts it in writing! Then she's laying her own head on the block."

"Well . . . All her life this woman has been a scandal to the Church. If she dies as a martyr for our cause, that will be the first useful thing she ever did for it."

"Then it's true. You do want Elizabeth to kill her."

"No, but if it happens — "

"This Babington plot — was it arranged on purpose for the Queen of Scots to embroil herself?"

"Really, Paul! There were none of us Jesuits in that Babington nonsense. The fellow who egged them on — what's his name?"

"Father Ballard."

"He was a secular priest, and entirely the French ambassador's creature."

"Then do the French want the Queen of Scots dead? Surely not. She's first cousin to the Duke of Guise."

"All the more reason for some people in France to hate her."

I said: "But at least it wasn't a Jesuit who tried to assassinate Elizabeth."

"Of course not. Those are children's games. Just because we brought it off once — when the Prince of Orange was justly executed by the only means available — we mustn't let success

138

go to our heads. To execute Elizabeth would not be enough to put things right. The only serious possibility of re-establishing the Church in England is the Spanish enterprise. Of course, there is one obstacle to that."

"Only one?"

"Yes; everything is arranged. It's just that the King of Spain can't make up his mind to move, so long as the Scottish woman is alive. Why should he invade in order to put her on the throne?"

I covered my face.

"Well, surely, Paul, if you think of it, this is obvious."

"It's obvious to Walsingham."

"What—that the Spaniards are going to invade? Knowing that in advance won't help him."

"What helps him is that he knows everything you do. He knows every code you write in; even his underlings can read your letters at sight. He knows that you want Elizabeth to kill the Queen of Scots. And he knows why. He arranged for poor little Sherwood to escape, so that he could bring you that reply from the Scottish Queen."

"What makes you think Sherwood brought it?"

"I know he did. I was there when he escaped. I told him not to go; it was all planned by Walsingham. Because Walsingham is always, always, one step ahead of you."

"How dare you!" shouted Parsons. "As your superior, I order you—"

"To do what?" I put in. "To stop telling you the truth?"

"As if it were the truth! I know by now when I'm hearing Walsingham's fables. This is an old story—that he knows everything, that he has more than human powers."

"Walsingham knows what people tell him—nothing else. But your letters tell him everything. He thinks you must intend that; he can't believe you'd be so careless—"

"Hold your tongue!"

"I was warned that word would make you angry. You'd rather be called a villain than careless. John Mush told me that."

"John Mush! You've been mixing with his kind! Who else? Christopher Bagshaw, I suppose."

"They were my fellow-prisoners for the Faith."

"Renegades! Traitors! Else why weren't they executed? Why should Walsingham keep those particular people alive?"

"Because he knows you want them dead. As you wanted me dead."

"What makes you think that?"

Angry as he was, he used the form of words which counts as equivocation, rather than a direct lie. I coldly pointed this out to him, and added: "When I came in just now, you started as if a ghost had come out of the grave to accuse you."

"You always were a lad with vivid fancies."

"Did I fancy it, when you said that the Queen of Scots could serve the cause best as a martyr? You thought the same of me. And of Robert Southwell."

"Robert Southwell! Your lover! You've been seeing him. I might have known."

"You sent him into Walsingham's hands. God's wind blew him out again. And Henry Garnett! Both of them would have been blessed martyrs for the Faith. You could have rolled up your eyes when you preached about them."

Parsons burst out: "How did you leave England?"

"First answer my question. Was it through carelessness or evil will that you sent me and Robert and Henry Garnett and Christopher Bagshaw into the very same trap?"

He went on shouting: "How did you leave England? How did you reach Rome so fast? Who paid your travelling expenses?"

"I left England by the same way I went in."

"Liar!"

"I travelled here with messengers from the Duke of Guise."

"Liar!"

"They paid my expenses and lent me a horse."

"Liar! Liar! Liar! Walsingham sent you! Confess it, Paul. Confess you're an agent of Walsingham. You'll find the Church can be very merciful. It can make allowance for your weakness, your cowardice . . ."

A Jesuit education is not to be despised. I kept my temper. He went on: "Only don't imagine that we don't know! We've been at it long enough; we know a renegade when we see one." He poked his face into mine and shrieked: "Confess it! You've been with women!"

I shook my head.

"We know it all — we know! Walsingham's been sending his men here, bribing cardinals, telling everybody how easy life would be for English Catholics, if only they'd give up their so-called plots."

Why *so-called*? I wondered silently.

He went on: "That would mean — give up every hope of power! And what are we offered in return? Toleration! Which would utterly destroy us!"

I said: "What about your pamphlet asking for liberty of conscience?"

"There's only one thing to do with you," said Parsons. "You must go into an enclosed monastery, and make a long retreat."

I shook my head. I was quite calm. I no longer had the torment of trying to believe that Parsons was a good man. The more he stormed, the less I had to regret. I told him quietly: "I cannot make a retreat. It is my duty, as a good Catholic, to go to the Pope and inform him of what you are doing."

Parsons thundered: "I am your superior, and I order you to make a retreat."

"I still refuse."

"Are you a Jesuit?"

"Are you? Have you obeyed the orders of General Aquaviva, to stop throwing lives away?"

He screamed at me: "Deserter!"

I replied in the words of young Nick. "To my way of thinking, the army's deserted me."

Then I made for the door. Parsons barred my way, threw a paper-knife to the floor, and began to shout: "Help! Murder!" When the servants came running he cried: "This madman is trying to kill me. Quick! Don't let him go!"

XII

THE TRUTH IS GREAT, and will prevail, but not immediately. While Parsons poured out fluent lies, I was dumbfounded. I found words again, plenty of words, but it was too late; I was alone, locked up in a dark room.

I rattled the door, stamped and shouted until I was tired. Then I reflected that this was hardly the way to convince the servants that I was not a madman.

I tried to pray. I wanted to ask for that calmness with which I had confronted Walsingham and Topcliffe. My prayers were disjointed, and calm did not come. Trembling, sweating, beating hand against hand, I wondered why.

I had known that Walsingham was an enemy. Defying him had been a simple matter, for which I was well prepared. Whereas Parsons was, as I had thought, my friend. Was this what confused me?

No. I had known for months – and could now admit – that in coming to see Parsons I was putting my head in the lion's mouth. The false accusation, the violence of the servants, the darkness of this new prison, though they had startled me, were not really unexpected.

Then why was I trembling as if a gulf had opened at my feet? I had been calm when Parsons revealed his nature, calm until . . .

I remembered it now. I had broken my vows. I had rejected an order from a superior. And I had heard words come out of my mouth which were not my own. "The army's deserted me!" What immeasurable insolence! I felt myself shaken through and through by pride, that the man who had taught me to speak like this was an Englishman.

I began to roam distractedly about the room. It was not, after all, completely dark. I could see chinks of light. They came from a window which was heavily shuttered. A pad-locked iron bar secured the shutters. Through a crack in the shutter I could see roofs, a wall, and another window, just as heavily shuttered.

I knew I was high up. "Lock him in the attic!" Parsons had screamed, and I remembered being dragged upstairs. How far up I did not know; I had struggled all the way, and sometimes rolled a little downwards, and they must have dragged me up the same stairs two or three times. It was only when I thought of this that I felt how badly I had been bruised.

The room was almost bare. Groping about, I found a chest, and a pisspot (which I was glad of) and a hard bed with one blanket — the sort of wretched blanket which is made only in Italy.

Dusk was falling. I became aware of the cold, and wrapped myself in the blanket, which might as well have been paper. I knew that I would grow steadily colder all night, since my belly was empty. Who, I wondered, was eating the Roman chicken, and drinking the wine from Frascati? I thought of Count Ugolino, starved to death in prison by an archbishop. According to Dante, the count spends eternity biting the back of the archbishop's neck. I did not want to spend eternity biting the back of Parson's neck. I did not think I would enjoy the taste.

Besides, it was my duty not to let him starve me, or

otherwise put me to silence. I had to return to England. I had to return to Anne.

At the word, her face appeared before me, bright as those visions the saints describe. I saw the majesty of those arched brows, and the cheeks' glowing, and the parting of the lips; and I waited for her to speak. But at once the vision was gone, and I could not call it back.

Yet it had brought me what I had been praying for — the power to consider my situation with calm.

Parsons had not expected to imprison me. The room he had found for the purpose was only an ordinary servant's room. The shutters were barred from within, to keep out clambering thieves. There must, then, be a gutter or drain by which a thief could approach.

I threw off the papery blanket, stood up, and began to examine the shutter, inch by inch, with my fingertips. There was no glass behind it. What came through the cracks was the midwinter wind. So I knew that I was at the back of the house. In Rome people set great store by "bella figura" — a good appearance — and they put glass in those windows that can be seen from the street.

The weakest part of the shutter was above the padlocked iron bar. This was a pity, but I reckoned that I could climb over the bar, if I stood on the chest. All I need do was make a big enough hole.

The knife I used to cut my meat had been taken away from me. I took off one shoe, and used the buckle to poke at the wood. In some places it gave easily. I pulled off chips with my fingers. I reckoned that by first light I would have at least a hole big enough to lean out of. I would see then what roofs and gutters were around me, what courtyards below. Meanwhile the work was hard enough to keep me almost warm.

After an hour or so I was interrupted by a noise behind me. Someone was unlocking the door. I hastily put on my shoe.

"I thought you might want something to eat," said Sir Francis. Men followed him, carrying candles, a glowing charcoal brazier, a small table and — after all! — some chicken, bread and wine. I told the servants to take the pisspot away, and bring me a bowl of warm water. Pretending not to be hungry, I refused to touch the food, until I had washed my hands. I was afraid that Sir Francis would see how dirty they were, and guess why. He might well see the damage I had done to the shutter, but he was sitting with his back to that, on the chest.

When the servants had left us alone, and I was eating, he said: "Well, Paul! I am sorry for this misunderstanding."

"There is no misunderstanding," I said. "I know the truth about Father Parsons, and he knows it, and is determined to keep me from telling the Pope."

"What on earth put it into your head," asked Sir Francis, "that the Pope does not know?"

"You did."

"When?"

"Before I went to England, you said that this new Pope did not care for Jesuits. You said he had stopped the subsidy to the English College. Parsons, you said, was finding doors locked in his face."

"Oh, but that was over a year ago. Now Pope Sixtus has come to appreciate the Jesuits."

"And yet it was when I said that I meant to appeal to the Pope – not before – that Parsons began to act that comedy for the servants."

"Nonsense, Paul! What put Father Parsons into such a combustion that . . . that, frankly, I don't think he knew quite what he was doing or saying . . . what grieved him to the soul was your breaking your vow of obedience. After all, quite apart from the difficulty – the impossibility – of a lad like you, without friends or money, making an appeal to the Pope, your vows as a Jesuit forbid you to make any such appeal."

"I have not made my final vows as a Jesuit."

"But your other vows, Paul! You are pledged to obey your superior without question."

"So I did once – and he sent me straight into the hands of Walsingham. To obey him again would be suicide, which is mortal sin."

I had not thought of this argument until I said it. Sir Franics greeted it with an admiring smile. "You can at least reason like a Jesuit!"

"I want to reason like a simple Catholic. I want to speak for those poor priests in England, who are continually in danger for the Faith. Parsons lives in safety and calls them renegades, traitors . . . Or, as he called me, a coward."

"Did he really say that? He was put out, you know, by your manner . . . And when you said that you'd come with Guise's men . . ."

"I did come with Guise's men."

"Yes; we know that now; we sent a message to the French ambassador's house. But we also know that Guise's men couldn't possibly have told you where to find Parsons. They don't know he's here. Hardly anyone does."

"Father Agazzari does."

"Agazzari! He told you?"

"Yes," I said, and added with some pleasure: "He knows where I am."

As I said this I reflected that it was not much comfort. A year before I had seen how completely Agazzari was under Parsons' thumb. If he were told that I was making a month's retreat, for prayer and meditation, he would not question further. And yet he might . . . I could see the same doubt flicker over Englefield's face. He leaned forward with a kindly smile.

"Of course, Paul, I know you're not a traitor. And certainly not a coward . . . Can't you finish your chicken? Is there anything else you fancy?"

I burst out laughing. He asked why. I said: "You remind me of someone I met in England."

I was thinking of the man in Colchester market place, who would get his friend to whip a dog, lock it up and starve it. Then he would come with food, and the dog would lick his hand . . . Did Sir Francis think I was as simple as a dog? He might. He had some reason. I said aloud: "I was a simpleton, when you sent me to England."

"Not at all!" said Sir Francis. "You were a very bright boy. That silversmith who took you to Paris — Minello — he said you were the best clerk he'd ever had. Hard-working, a fluent interpreter, always ready with a song to cheer him up. You had a rough journey through France, I believe."

"Coming and going, I've had *two* rough journeys through France. I've seen what a religious war is like."

"Paul, you know as well as I do why that bloodshed in France has dragged on. It's because the Guises — and the Catholics in general — have been too shy about asking the King of Spain for his help. The Spanish army could finish it in a month."

"They're taking a bit longer in the Low Countries."

"They'd finish that off tomorrow, if all they had to contend with were Elizabeth's army. She made herself ridiculous, letting her old lover take that gang of jailbirds to Zutphen. Ran away at the first assault . . . What Elizabeth's done is to show how easy the conquest of England is going to be."

"Are you sure that the Spanish army can reach England?"

"Come, Paul, you may not like the prospect, but you needn't raise ridiculous objections. You're seeing things out of proportion. Just because old Parsons has been a bit hard on you . . . Between ourselves, his trouble is — he can't bear a young man to be good-looking."

I remembered the last time Sir Francis had said this to me. I said: "Before I left Rome, I asked Parsons for his blessing. And then you said: 'I need a blessing too. I need it more, because my part is the hardest.' Did you mean — because you had it on your conscience, that I was being sent on purpose to be captured?"

"On purpose? Who can say that?"

"I'm saying it."

"Well, if you know which of old Parsons' mistakes *are* mistakes, and which are the outcome of some devious design, you know more than anyone else does. Including himself. Because, once a mistake has happened, he'll never admit that it was a mistake. He'll always find some far-fetched reason why he meant things to turn out like that."

"So . . . perhaps he didn't really want Elizabeth to execute the Queen of Scots. Only, now that it's inevitable . . ."

"Mind you, that's Parsons' great strength. Every new disaster sets him looking for some new advantage to be won. He's cheerfully torn up the pamphlet he was writing, to prove that the Queen of Scots was the rightful Queen of England. He's writing another one, to show that the King of Spain is descended from Edward the Third."

"I'm descended from Edward the Third."

"Oh, so am I. So are half the gentlefolk of England. But you and I, Paul, can't bring armies into the field."

"Does the King of Spain mean to seize the English throne for himself?"

"He has promised the Pope that the English people will be allowed to choose who their king should be."

"Choose? With Spanish pikes at their throats?"

"The Pope will send his emissaries to see that the choice is fairly and freely made."

"You mean that this is what you're telling the Pope? Knowing that King Philip intends to seize the throne for himself, long before these emissaries can come from Rome."

"I said you were a bright boy."

"But the purpose of this invasion is to bring England back to its ancient obedience to the Pope. Now you prepare for it by lying to the Pope."

"Not lying, Paul — equivocating a little. The Pope, you see, does not want us to put it too plainly. He wants to go on telling the other Catholic rulers, who are jealous of Spain, that this is not an ordinary war of conquest."

"Do you think that the Faith can be served by all this plotting and lying?"

"Of course it can. You accepted that, when you became a Jesuit."

"No!"

"Come now, Paul! Your beloved Possevino – did he always tell the truth to those Russians?"

I thought of Possevino, saying: "We must be a little economical with truth." I thought of his messenger going ahead to ensure that the Russians would have a completely misleading view of every church and monastery where they stayed. I thought of myself, deceiving the Russians in order to compose a pamphlet in their language against their faith. I could not answer Englefield. He saw his advantage, and pursued it. "Didn't I myself arrange, at your request, that they should be bribed with silks and velvets to outrage their own religion?"

Still I could not answer him. He went on: "And, Paul, this obedience you swore to – wasn't this your way of making sure that other people obeyed you? If Possevino had gone to Russia, and you beside him, wouldn't you be like the Jesuits in India or Japan? Wouldn't you show simple people your medicines and your clocks, and use every cheap device to win fame as a magician? You'd have those barbarians eating out of your hand. Because that's the advantage of belonging to a great army. You have to be obedient – yes! – but you yourself have immeasurable power."

I shook my head.

"Oh yes, Paul. What you want is power. And why not? It's yours. Because you're not what you make out. Not a simple boy, led astray by scheming superiors. You've shown today that you have the stuff in you to *be* a superior. Now, if you join the other English Jesuits, Father Cresswell and Father Holt, who are preparing to sail in the Spanish fleet, you'll be where you ought to be. Among the rulers of England."

Here, at last, I said: "No."

He gave me a kindly smile, and a shake of the head, as if meaning that when I had thought the matter over I would see reason. Then he went to the door, and called the servants to take away what was left of the meal. As he turned his back I took the knife, which had been given me to cut the chicken, and slipped it into a crevice of the bed where I sat. The servants came reluctantly, and yawning, too sleepy to see that the knife was missing.

"You see, Paul," said Sir Francis, "this great enterprise is coming, and you can't prevent it. But if you decide to work for it, heart and soul . . ."

I asked: "What will happen if I decide otherwise?"

"A period of meditation," he said, preparing to lock the door, "is good for the soul."

"I shall meditate better if I have blankets with a bit of warmth in them. And sheets. And another brazier — this one is almost cold."

"I think – not sheets," he said. "You lads have been taught to make ropes out of sheets. But blankets, if you like, and a fresh brazier."

The servants brought these things. Before he locked the door, Sir Francis murmured: "I suppose, Paul, there is nothing in what old Parsons thinks? If there were a woman behind all this . . ."

"Good night!" I said. "I shall think over your arguments."

I did think them over, while I worked on the shutter. I could get on much faster, now that I had a knife. I heated it from time to time in the brazier, so that, without setting the wood alight, it made a series of charred indentations. Long before dawn, I had a respectable hole.

I stood on the chest and looked out. What lay below me was a well of blackness. I surmised, rather than saw, that it was an enclosed courtyard. If I got safely down, I had still to get through the house. Perhaps when the kitchen boy got up to light the braziers . . .

If a rope could be made of sheets, why not of blankets? I soon discovered why not. The thin blanket I had had at first was easy enough to tear into strips. But when I began to tie the strips together I found that they also tore crosswise — that is, my rope was breaking before I had put any weight upon it.

The other blankets were thicker, but not a great deal stronger. Who has ever made a rope of wool?

I sat with my failed ropes about me, thinking. If I were "a

simple boy, led astray by cunning superiors," I would tie the blankets together as best I might, slide down them, fall, break my leg, and be carried ignominiously back into the house. But Englefield had told me that I was not simple. I was myself a schemer, and I wanted power.

I had been sitting on the hard mattress of my bed. Now I jumped up, and began to rip the cover. That at least would not be made of wool. Certainly it was a hard material, and as I ripped it with my knife I made more noise than with anything else I had done.

I heard someone stir outside, and a key turn in the lock. Holding the knife ready for my defence, I darted behind the door.

A servant came in carrying a torch. It was at once blown out by the cold air from the hole I had made in the shutter. My labour in making that hole had not been in vain, because the man ran to look out of it, and I was able to seize him from behind.

He was a little fellow, this poor servant they had set outside my door to listen. I towered above him. I held one hand over his mouth, and, with the other, pointed my knife at his throat. Sir Francis was right; I did feel it as a pleasure to have power over someone.

I whispered to him: "Show me the way to the front door, and unlock it for me. Keep quiet, and I won't do you any harm."

Would I have done him any harm if he had refused? I shall always be grateful to him, that he did not put me to that test.

We crept down the stairs in dead silence. But he could not open the front door quietly. Chains and bolts grated, then clattered, while I looked up the stairs, holding the knife ready for the first man down.

I heard people stirring. There was a step on the stairs. But now the door was open, and I was out.

Parsons would look for me first at the English College. I ran the other way. There was one place in Rome where I could be out of Parsons' reach. Dodging through lanes and alleys, I came to the French ambassador's house, and pounded upon the gate.

The porter was very unwilling to let me in. My hair, my beard and my black Jesuit's robe were covered with blanket fluff. Worse, my hands, which I had cut two or three times as I worked on the shutter, were caked with dirt and blood. I told the porter: "I have been attacked by ruffians." (Which was true enough.) "I have an urgent message for Monsieur Delahaye."

Once he had let me in, I did not care how long he made me wait. There was a pump in the yard; I staggered up to it and began trying to wash off the blood. Then a maid took pity on me and bandaged my hands, and put something cool over one eye. I had not known I had a black eye, but now I could feel it throbbing. My other bruises from the struggle of the night before had also come to life.

I looked a little more decent when I was shown into the room where M. Delahaye was having breakfast. As the windows were shuttered he could scarcely see me, but he knew who I was.

"My dear Father Calverley," he said coldly, "I really have very little time. The Pope is going to receive me this morning. I wish you would tell Father Parsons not to pester me with his 'urgent messages.' If you must know, the truth is that my master, the Duke of Guise, does not mean to burn his fingers in any more of Parsons' plots."

I said: "I have run away from Father Parsons. He tried to keep me prisoner. Please give me shelter here."

"But if you've quarrelled with Parsons, why can't you go to the English? Of course, your Queen has no ambassador here. But there is an envoy of sorts . . ."

"I have not come to that," I said. "To take refuge with Protestants . . . In spite of what my fellow-Catholics have done to me."

"Why—what have they done to you?"

He called a servant to open the shutters, and saw for the first time my black eye and my bandaged hands. "My God! Are you the same young man . . . ? Why did you say that Parsons was angry with you?"

I told him. He said: "The ambassador ought to hear this."

The French ambassador said, when he had heard it: "But everyone in Europe knows that Parsons is a Spanish agent. Do you mean to say that you have only just found out?"

However, he agreed to shelter me. He and M. Delahaye were to see the Pope together; they were willing to give His Holiness a letter which I now hastened to write.

In this letter I said simply what I knew of Parsons. The ambassador advised me not yet to ask for a dispensation from my vows. For this he found me someone skilled in canon law.

The lawyer told me that I might be released from my vows, if I could prove that I had taken them in error. He helped me to draw up an affidavit, showing how I had been misled as to the purpose of the English mission. The French, in order to discredit Spain, would gladly put this before the Papal Courts. "But I am afraid," the lawyer added, "that you will get no decision for at least a year."

I could not spend a year in idleness. I wrote to Father Aquaviva, General of the Society of Jesus. I admitted that until I was released my vows bound me, and that I had therefore done wrong to disobey Father Parsons. "But I did it to avoid a greater sin — suicide. I am only one of numerous priests whom Father Parsons has delivered into mortal danger." Then I wrote down a list I had long carried in my head — the list of those priests I knew, and by each one's name the number of days (or hours) he had remained at liberty in England. I described the accident by which Father Garnett and Father Southwell had avoided capture. I added that I meant to return to England, and thought I might remain at liberty there, since I would use a landing-place unknown to Parsons. In England my superior would be Father Garnett, whose orders I could obey with a good conscience.

Putting this resolution into practice was not easy. The French ambassador could have no part in smuggling me to

England. "Since that Babington business our man in London has been watched night and day."

I wrote to the silversmith Minello, with whom I had travelled before. He was almost illiterate, and had no thoughts beyond his beloved forks, and the money they brought him. I would never have thought of writing to him, if Englefield had not reported him as praising me.

I scarcely expected Minello to answer. I had had no replies from General Aquaviva, or the Pope, and the canon lawyer had vanished into the mazes of the Vatican. But Minello, a few minutes after my letter reached him, came bounding into the French ambassador's house. He called me "Paolo mio" and whispered that he had really always known I was a priest. "Because you used to turn away, and blush, when the rest of us were telling stories." But he had not known I was English. "You talk just like I do — that is, better, because you've been to school."

I was not sure how to explain that I had fallen foul of my Jesuit superior. But Minello accepted this at once. "Of course all good Catholics hate the Jesuits!" He was sorry that I meant to go back to England. Could I not stay, and be his clerk again, and perhaps, in time, his partner? I wished that this were possible. After being among people who professed themselves religious, to be with him was like warming frozen hands.

When he saw that I was set on returning to my own country, he grew thoughtful. He had long dreamed, he said, of sending his forks to England. "That's where the money is now! But I had nobody I could trust to be my agent in London. In my business, I'm so easily robbed. Do you know, Paolo mio, you are the only man I've employed who never took so much as a shaving of silver. Now, if you could take some of my forks, and show them at the English court . . . Why, if Queen Elizabeth could be persuaded to eat her meat with a fork, the whole English nation would follow her!"

There was a simple recklessness about this plan which pleased me. To walk into Elizabeth's court, to come face to face, perhaps, with Walsingham . . . At least this time I would be choosing my own trap.

Once I said yes, Minello bounced into action. He had a false passport made for me, in an Italian name. He sent me a tailor, who fitted me out with Italian clothes. He provided a hair dye of such quality that, so long as I used it regularly, nobody could tell that I had not been born dark.

"Only . . . only there is one thing, Paolo mio. Going through France, in the fighting—that's altogether too risky. The ships take the long way round, by Spain. So you'll be about six weeks at sea."

XIII

GOD ORDAINED OTHERWISE. Or Sir Francis Drake did.
When I reached Barcelona, in May, 1587, I learned that it was
impossible to use the Atlantic ports of Spain. Drake had
wrecked the Spanish fleet in Cadiz harbour, had seized a castle
near Cape St. Vincent, and was now patrolling all the western
Spanish coast, intercepting every ship which tried to trade
there.

The ship I was on turned and made for Marseilles. Instead
of lamenting the setback, the Italian captain and crew laughed
heartily at the humiliation of Spain. It gave them hope, they
said, that the Spaniards could be driven even out of Southern
Italy.

At Marseilles I supervised the unloading of Minello's goods
on to pack-horses. The other merchants on the ship agreed
that we should all make for Bordeaux. So long as we kept
together, and took it in turns to watch the pack-horses day and
night, we should be safe.

So we were, from robbers, but not from persistent beggars.
There were wandering children, orphaned by the war, turned

wild as wolves. The girls without shame offered us their bodies; the boys threatened to bite us and thereby (they said) infect us with the pox. At this third view of poor France's misery, I could not help thanking God for Drake.

From Bordeaux we sailed for Southampton, where I landed safely, speaking broken English and showing the papers which described me as an Italian. It was as well they were in order; as I rode to London I had to show them again and again. I was on a good horse, and looked like a gentleman, but this was no longer enough. England had altered. Drake had by now returned from Cadiz in triumph. But the Spanish fleet could not again be taken completely by surprise. It would reassemble, and attack next year. Englishmen were preparing, and they did not want foreigners to see their preparations. I rode without pausing past a village green, where some squire was teaching country lads how horses are used in war. The squire himself seemed to have had some practice — perhaps he had been with Leicester in the Low Countries — but the rustics' clumsiness was empurpling him with rage. I heard him yell: "Don't any of you know your right hand from your left?"

I dared not laugh. Indeed, I did not want to. Above the stumbling horsemen rose a wooded hillside. Oak and beech, all heavy with late summer, brooded about the scene. The hedges were full of blackberries, as tasty and succulent as in Italy they would have been insipid and dry. The last harvest wagons were trundling by unguarded; there were no soldiers to attack them. I had never loved my country more.

Since Minello's forks were worth some hundreds of pounds, my first concern in London was to find a goldsmith with whom I could leave them securely. Having accomplished this, I went in search of a pork butcher called Foscue.

Although I had known him and all his family, while I was in the Clink, I had never seen his house. I knew it was near Smithfield, and I asked up and down, never for a moment forgetting my broken English, or my pose as a foreigner.

People told me that they did not know the Foscue family, had never heard of them . . . At last one old woman shouted:

"Who are you, then, to come here, making out we're friends with traitors?"

I said: "Not understand." Keeping it up, I went on: "Someone tell me – want good pork pies, go to Mr. Foscue of Smithfield. What is this word – traitors?"

"Oh. Well, what I mean – they ran away."

"Ran away? Where?"

"How should I know? Don't you dare to say I know! Never told me they was going. Never told any of us. We woke up one morning – the house was empty."

By this time the neighbours were in a circle round us. Someone was asking: "Why was the beadle so easy with 'em, this long time? We all knew they never went to church."

Another woman said: "You know what I reckon? I reckon they knew they was for it, once that young girl was taken."

I repeated slowly: "A young girl?"

"Oh, a girl they had living with 'em. She's in prison for helping a priest to escape."

I could not find out which prison. "Somewhere up north, was it?" they asked each other. I said laboriously: "So – I find no pork pies!" At this they all became quite friendly, pointing out the way to another butcher. "It's just round there, and then *across*, you know, and up the alley – not the blind alley, the other one – and then you go *round*, and it's the fourth – no, the fifth . . . Everybody knows. You can't miss it."

I did miss it, however, and went to the Strand, to Arundel House, where I asked for Mr. Cotton.

For a moment Robert Southwell did not recognise me. When he did, he almost burst into tears. "Oh, Paul, what a shame! Your beautiful hair . . ."

I cut him short, begging for news of Anne.

"She's in Lancaster Castle. Nobody's allowed to see her."

"Nobody at all?"

"Only her father. He's trying to persuade her to go to church."

"And she refuses?"

"She must be refusing still. Else they'd have let her out."

"I must see her. Perhaps Christopher could think of a way. Where is Christopher Bagshaw now?"

"In Wisbech Castle."

"And John Mush?"

"Oh, he's free still. He came here once. He wants me to print his pamphlet about Margaret Clitheroe. But whether I should . . . There's all this doubtful stuff in it. About a Puritan speaking up for her in court."

"Yes, that really happened."

"Oh it may have *happened*, but . . . English Catholics are still very confused; we don't want to confuse them further. Things are so much worse now than when you left! Elizabeth's breaking her own laws. She keeps arresting our people and holding them without a trial."

"Aren't they safer like that? If Anne were put on trial, the jury would convict her. People seem far more bitter against us now."

"Yes; it's all this nonsense about plots. That was the pretext for murdering poor Queen Mary of Scotland. I wrote a poem about that. Would you like to see it?"

"Very much."

Robert's poem depicted the Queen of Scots as a martyr, dying joyously for the Faith. One verse ran:

> Rue not my death, rejoice at my repose,
> It was no death to me but to my woe,
> The bud was opened to let out the rose,
> The chains unloosed to let the captive go.

I wanted to kneel down and kiss his feet. I wanted to tell him that the facts were otherwise. I did neither, because it came to me that Anne might die in prison, only for helping me. I burst into tears.

"Cheer up!" Robert said. "The heretics won't have it all their own way. Look, I've printed a new pamphlet . . ."

I glanced at the pamphlet, and saw the lines: "We Jesuits do not help the King of Spain to make war against Her Majesty, and we defy anyone to prove the assertion that we contribute to the Spanish fleet."

"Oh, Robert, Robert!" I said. "When the Spanish fleet sails — if it ever does — it will be carrying two English Jesuits, Cresswell and Holt."

"Oh, I know that."

"You *know*?"

"Yes. You see in the pamphlet I don't say it isn't so. I defy them to prove it. Which of course they can't do until the Spaniards land here, and then they'll be in no condition to prove anything."

"But what about this part? 'We Jesuits do not help the King of Spain to make war against Her Majesty.'"

"I haven't said *which* Majesty. I mean the Queen Mother of France."

"For God's sake, Robert — can't you see that this equivocation is what gives Jesuits a bad name?"

"Whatever we do we'll have a bad name among the heretics."

"But it's honest Catholics . . ." I told my story.

Robert listened quietly until I came to the point where I had disobeyed Parsons. Then he cried out: "How could you, Paul? Parsons was your lawful superior."

"But he's also a very wicked man."

"That makes no difference."

"Robert, do you honestly mean that?"

"Of course. Else where's our discipline? If we choose for ourselves what orders we obey, and from whom, we'll be back where we started. Why, when Ignatius Loyola first came to Rome, the Pope was ordering all bishops back to their sees. They simply didn't go. They had an easier life in Rome. The Pope ordered them again. They still didn't go. And that's what the Church used to be like! No wonder Luther almost overturned it! God's given the Church one more chance; he's given it through the Society of Jesus. We're an army — "

"Part of the Spanish army."

"Well, for the moment. Because, as things are, the King of Spain is acting as God's instrument."

"Robert, when you came to see me in the Clink, you said you had assured Parsons that you wouldn't mention politics in England."

"Yes. Meaning, of course—until I was quite sure who I was talking to."

"Did Parsons know you meant that?"

"I think so."

"I think he didn't. I think he considered you the kind of innocent fool I was. I think he gave you orders which were intended to lead to your capture."

"No!"

"Robert, the men waiting for you at Newhaven actually knew your name. And Henry Garnett's."

"Even if they did . . . There are spies for Walsingham in Rome, in Rouen . . ."

"Spies, yes—but Parsons makes it easy for them."

"He doesn't! That is, if he did, this time, it must have been due to a misunderstanding. Father Garnett was very slow—he admits this himself—he was very reluctant to see that the Spanish enterprise would be necessary. I know Father Parsons was rather impatient with him."

"Then you're saying what I'm saying—that if Parsons believes a priest isn't heart and soul for Spain, he sends him into the hands of Walsingham."

"No! It's not like that!"

"Then what is it like?"

"We can't pry into all the motives of our superiors. We can't see every device and every tactic that they make use of to confuse the enemy. Perhaps they may sometimes decide to sacrifice a small part of their own troops for the sake of the rest. All I know is—if that's my superior in front of me, giving me an order, I must obey."

"But if he's at odds with his own superior—"

"If he's at odds with an angel from Heaven, and the angel comes down to tell me so, I still have to obey my superior. That's the vow I took. And a vow is a sacred thing."

"The vows of marriage are sacred. But a man may have his

marriage annulled, if he finds that his bride was pregnant by another man. When we took our vows our superiors' minds were pregnant with a number of things they kept secret."

"How can you make such a disgusting comparison?" Robert was now in tears. "To talk as if our superiors were *women* . . ."

It was time to go. The next day I began my journey to the North.

XIV

THE WORST PART WAS the approach to Wisbech Castle. I
dared not for an instant seem an Englishman, but how could
I bring trouble on my old companions, by letting it appear that
they had foreign visitors?

Perhaps, though, my foreign pose was for the best. Elizabeth's law called it treason for us English Catholics, "Her
Majesty's natural subjects", to acknowledge the Pope's
authority. But this could not be treason in a foreigner.

I rode straight up to Wisbech Castle and insisted on seeing
the keeper, one Thomas Gray. I showed him some silver forks.
Might I present him with a couple? He preferred to take
money. Then I explained that, as an Italian, I was naturally a
Catholic. I felt great need of confession and absolution. Might
I confess to one of his prisoners?

He laughed. "Take your pick! Jesuit or secular? They're
separate breeds; they won't even eat together."

"Secular!" I said, and he led me into the hall where about a
dozen priests were finishing their dinner. I recognised my old
companions among them. "Is here ze Cattolic priests?" I
asked. "*Chi parla italiano?*"

Several voices answered, but I picked out Christopher. Mr. Gray allowed me to go with him to a quiet corner. "I shall have to sit over here and watch you," Mr. Gray said. "That's the rule. But it's all right; I shan't understand a word you say."

I knelt down by Christopher. Peering through my blackened beard, he whispered: "Is it really you? . . . I wasn't sure at first; your Italian accent . . . It might be old Agazzari talking. And that hair dye . . . The person who disguised you this time knew what he was doing."

I told him about Minello and the forks.

"Then you have a perfect reason for going about the country? And good papers? And money? But what about a servant, Paul? If you go alone, aren't you afraid of being robbed?"

I said: "Nowadays people don't carry great sums of money. The goldsmiths in most English towns will honour letters of credit from Italian bankers."

"What a cunning device! Can't you persuade this illiterate fork-maker to take charge of the English mission?"

I told Christopher what had happened in Rome, and begged his forgiveness for having doubted his word. He whispered: "Can *you* forgive *me*, for sending you into such danger? Thank God we have a Pope who doesn't like the Jesuits! If old Gregory were still in the Papal chair, I don't believe you'd have left Rome alive."

"I'm not sure that Pope Sixtus dislikes Jesuits. He didn't answer my letter."

"No, I wouldn't expect him to. He's under the thumb of the Spaniards. Not that he wants to be, but France is torn apart, and the German Emperor thinks of nothing but horses and dogs, and Spain looks like the one great Catholic power."

"So my appeal to the Pope was useless."

"No. It will be remembered, if the Spaniards are defeated."

"And if they win . . ."

"Oh, if they win, we'll take up the appeal in Paradise. They'll hang you and me before anyone. What a lot of people want to hang us, Paul! With so many dangers, you'd better make your confession in earnest."

I did. I told him that I wanted a dispensation from my vows, so that I could marry Anne.

He sighed. "Did you put that in writing?"

"Not . . . not the part about marriage. The canon lawyer told me I had grounds enough to obtain a dispensation."

"I doubt it. Besides, they'll guess it's for marriage. It always is. Oh, Paul! If this gets out it may make things harder for us. You don't know what's been happening here, in Wisbech."

"Is it true the Jesuits won't eat with you?"

"That's right. This Jesuit Weston — the man who casts out evil spirits — has been treating us all as if we were evil spirits. It's really because of Sir William Stanley."

"Who?"

"One of Leicester's officers in the Low Countries. A Catholic. Last winter he betrayed the town of Deventer to the Spaniards. Now Parsons' friend William Allen has written a pamphlet to prove he was right. Because the Queen is a heretic and we all ought to disobey her. The Queen sent a man to read us parts of this pamphlet, and ask us if we agreed with it. Of course we seculars all said 'No' outright."

"What did the Jesuits say?"

"They said they couldn't eat with us; we were always chasing women. They'd be so pleased, Paul, if they knew you really were! I wished you hadn't mixed your own desires with a good cause."

"They're both good causes. The Church would have been saved innumerable scandals if more priests had been willing to admit that they had no vocation."

"I've never met a priest with more vocation than you. As the miller said, it's written in your face. Besides, what makes you think Anne Clitheroe would have you? Did she say anything?"

"When we parted, she kissed me."

"That's a good old English custom."

"Now, because of me, she's imprisoned in Lancaster Castle."

"No. She's gone home to York, to her father."

I sprang to my feet.

"Wait!" shouted Christopher — and hastily added: "*Aspetta!*" for Mr. Gray was watching us narrowly. In Italian, Christopher told me to kneel down again. "I haven't absolved you yet. And I ought not to absolve you, if you're going to York for more kisses."

"I only want to see her face."

"Do you promise not to touch her, unless the Church releases you from your vows?"

"Yes, I promise that."

He sighed heavily, but sent me away with his blessing.

Four miles from York I turned aside, into a lane I knew. Harvest was over. But some apples hung, still, on the familiar trees. The fish-ponds reflected a warm sky; the fat cabbages and beans had not yet felt the first nip of the frost. I put out my hand, and felt the brick wall my grandfather had built. The sun had left it, but it was warm to the touch, as if it welcomed me home.

My home . . . I prayed that I might not bring disaster on it. But why should I? There was not a servant or farm hand who had set eyes on me, since I was fourteen years old.

We cannot foresee everything. My mother knew me, and fainted; and the maid who was with her guessed why. "But the girl is a good Catholic!" whispered my mother. "All our servants are."

I said: "Where's father?"

"Oh, my dear! Forty miles away. At Scarborough, drilling the trained bands, in case the Spaniards land there."

"They won't this year."

"Yes, but we have to be ready. Especially Catholics. We have to do more than other people, to prove we're loyal. But, Paul, your dad will be back with us in ten days."

"I can't spend more than one night anywhere." Then I explained about the forks. "They give me a good reason for visiting gentlefolk's houses. But I daren't go to the Shambles in York and visit a butcher. Nobody would believe that Mr. Clitheroe was learning to eat with a fork."

"No, and he wouldn't let you in. He's been so harried on poor Margaret's account, he swears he'll never speak to a stranger again, for fear it's a priest in disguise."

"Then how am I to see Anne?"

"I will bring her to you," said my mother.

The next morning she set out with her maid. The maid was to stay in York, to do Anne's work in the house; otherwise her father would never allow her the outing. "And even then," said my mother, "I'll be half the day persuading the old grumblepot."

In fact she was not so long. Within two hours, I looked through the shutters of my attic hiding-place, and saw Anne riding into our orchard, with a little boy on her saddle-bow. The boy jumped down and ran to help the men picking the apples. Anne stayed a moment in the saddle, and looked up, as if she could see me, though she could not. The autumn sunlight was on her face; for that moment it was as I had seen it in my vision.

But when she came into the attic that brightness was muddied with tears. She sank at my feet, wailing: "Oh, Father Calverley! How can I face you? I am ashamed, ashamed!"

I said: "Why? Anne, what have you done?"

She only sobbed more desperately.

I shouted: "For God's sake, what is it? Did you let a man — "

"Oh, no, no!" she cried out. "That was my sister!"

Only then did I become aware that I was not standing with dignity, like a priest receiving a penitent. I was kneeling on the floor, face to face with her, gripping her wrist so hard that her face was distorted with pain.

So already I had broken my promise not to touch her. I was terrified of what I might do next. I dropped Anne's wrist — the marks of my fingers glared on her skin — and scrambled to my feet. She was now moaning: "Oh, Father Calverley, how could you think that of me?"

167

I echoed: "Yes, how could I?" What was this feeling which had brought me to my knees? And now why was I (even while I composed myself, and sat waiting for Anne's confession) trembling with happiness?

She had not let another man possess her. She might have committed every other deadly sin; I did not care. And still I shrank from giving a name to my feeling. I looked into Anne's face — now lifted up to mine, but at a decorous distance — and loved it more because it was not beautiful. The tear-swollen eyes and reddened nose told me that my accusation had hurt her. I felt remorse for this, but also gladness. I could not have endured it, if she had remained calm. She must be made to feel what I felt. And what I felt . . . I had heard other people confess it, but those were other people. Surely my own breast could not be filled with jealousy?

She was beginning: "Father, I have sinned . . ."

I stopped her. "Anne, it's not right I should hear your confession as a priest. I have asked the Church to release me from my vows."

"But why?"

"I am not good enough to be a priest."

She cried out: "But nobody is better than you!"

"John Mush is. You might confess to him."

"Oh, if only I could! He sent me a message to say that it would be his death and mine, if he came to York again. Which is true, of course. They've been watching for him ever since they killed my mother."

"Then haven't you been able to see a priest at all?"

"Only an old one, from Queen Mary's time."

"Don't say 'only'. Those old people, Anne, were born when everyone was Catholic. It's like breathing to them. They aren't fierce and bitter in the cause, like us. Maybe that's best. Your old priest may have given you good advice."

"But he wouldn't tell me that what I did was wrong!"

I said: "So you've already been absolved. Get off your knees. Go and sit there, where I can see your face. And talk to me, Anne, like a friend. Because you are my truest and best friend. You set me free. What did they do to you, Anne, after that?"

"Oh, nothing much. They only asked me where you were. I said I didn't know. That wasn't quite a lie, was it? Because I really didn't know if you'd reached Mrs. Wiseman safely, or if you'd gone on from there to another house . . . Well, they couldn't prove I knew. Only they said it looked bad, that I was in the same inn. And I was travelling with just one maid. They said that wasn't modest. And then, after saying that one maid wasn't enough, they wouldn't let me have a maid at all. They sent her back to Mrs. Foscue. Poor Mrs. Foscue! I wonder where she is now."

"Anne, what did they do to you, when they had you alone?"

"Well, first they put me in prison at Cambridge."

"The common prison?"

"Yes, among some . . . some rough women. But *they* never did me any harm. I helped them, you see, to tidy the prison, and clean it, and then we were all more comfortable. So one morning, when I was teaching them to sing descants — "

"You taught those women to sing?"

"Yes. They said it made a change, a bit of music. The prison keeper didn't like it, though. He came to me that morning and said: 'Good riddance! You're to go to Lancaster Castle.'"

"How did they take you there?"

"On a horse. Oh, but not tied on. They tried to tie me to the side-saddle, but it all kept slipping, so in the end they let me ride as I liked. It was a beautiful journey, through Derbyshire, and the hills. I was singing, all the way. And then, at Lancaster Castle, men came to ask me again where you were. That was a whole month after you'd escaped. So I knew you must be gone across the seas. And I felt certain Father Mush would be safe; he knows every hiding-place in England. I was so happy! Only . . . only then they let my father visit me."

Her voice faltered. I asked her gently: "He's a Protestant?"

"But he is my father! And my mother always told me to love

169

him and obey him. Just as we have to obey a Protestant queen."

"Your mother was right."

"Well, at first I was quite clear and certain. I told my father I'd obey him as I obeyed the Queen — that is, I would do anything but go to church. He said that was the only thing I could do that would get me out of prison. And he needed me at home, he said; my little brothers and sisters were getting out of hand. He made me cry, talking of home . . . But I didn't weaken. I didn't weaken then. Because, every time I thought why I was in prison — every time I thought of you — I blessed the very bars."

I put out my hands towards her, and then remembered, and firmly folded my arms.

She went on: "A month later, though, my father came again. He said: 'I told you the young ones were out of hand.' And . . . and then he told me about my sister. Fourteen years old, and he had to marry her off in a hurry, to one of his own apprentices. And the young man wouldn't even take her — stood there with a face of brass and said it might be some other fellow's doing — until my father bought him a shop of his own. And that cost my poor dad so much money that he had to send all the servants back to their families, bar one orphan girl who had no family but ours. He said to me: 'I can't blame you, not wanting to come home. As well be in prison as do that rough kitchen work.' When he said that I did begin to weaken. Can you understand?"

"Yes, I understand."

"And then there was this old priest they brought into the prison. He was only there waiting for someone to pay his fine for saying Mass. He wasn't threatened with death. And that's another thing! How can these old priests be any good, if the Government never troubles to put them to death?"

"That would be against English law — to punish a man for something that wasn't a crime when he did it. They became priests when it was legal. The law that threatens us young priests is cruel and unjust, but we were given warning of it."

"But they're altogether so different, these old men! They don't seem like priests at all. I asked this one what he thought I ought to do, and he said: 'Why, you silly girl, go to church!' And then he said: 'They don't worship the Devil or Beezlebub in there. It's only our Catholic liturgy, done into English!' And he promised to hear my confession afterwards. And so I ... I did it."

"You went to church, Anne? Was that really all you did?"

"But it was mortal sin! I've heard you say that often."

"Perhaps I was wrong ... Besides, it would have been a sin to leave your brothers and sisters when they were in so much trouble."

She shook her head. "Since I've been home I've wished a thousand times that I were back in prison."

I looked at her hands. They were red as a washerwoman's.

"You've been scrubbing hard," I said.

"Oh, it's not the work. It's not even the want of sleep. Poor little Harry" — she pointed out at the orchard, where the little boy was chattering too loudly, on too high a note — "he wakes every night screaming, and I have to rock him asleep again. But it isn't that. What's hard, what's terrible, is the talk of the people."

"They talk about your sister?"

"It's worse than that. You see, my mother's trouble was all because her stepfather had a spite against her. Last year he was Lord Mayor of York. It was his doing they searched our house. After my mother was put to death he had her buried by a dung-hill. Even the people who'd been against her thought that was wrong; they jeered at him in the streets. Then he put it about that Father Mush had been my mother's lover. He said the reason she refused to plead was that, if there'd been a trial, there would have been evidence given of her adultery."

"Don't cry, Anne. People everywhere take pleasure in saying such things. You know that your mother was a good mother. I'm sure your father knows that she was a good wife."

"Oh yes; father tells everyone that. 'The best wife a man could have,' he says, 'for all her notions.' But then, when my little sister was married, people jeered at her big belly, and called out: 'Like mother, like daughter.' And it doesn't die down. It gets worse."

"Oh, Anne, surely not."

"That wicked man — her stepfather — when he sees that people are tired of hearing one lie, he tells them another. He says now that my mother had monstrous, perverse desires. And anything that we do wrong — we, her children — will make people believe him. I tell my other sisters: we're poor; the whole town is against us; we have nothing now but our good name. If we lose that we blacken her name too."

She could not with more force have pleaded for her chastity. It was this, not my vows, not my promise to Christopher, that held me back.

The child outside began a sort of grating wail that set my teeth on edge. Anne ran to the window and called: "Harry, Harry, give over! I'm coming!"

I said: "Wait! Anne, it may be a year or more. But when the Church releases me from my vows, I will come to see you again."

"Do you promise that?"

"I do."

We parted, and, this time, without a kiss. It was for good and honourable reasons that I failed to take my darling in my arms.

XV

I RETURNED TO LONDON, and began to sell Minello's forks
in earnest. I had to. How else would I be able to support myself and Anne?

Though I never came face to face with Walsingham, or the
Queen, I did find customers among the great men of the court.
Their wives were entranced to learn that Italian ladies' hands
were as clean at the end of a meal as at the beginning. Soon it
was the height of fashion to hold a banquet with a fork as well
as a knife laid ready for each guest. At the New Year several
noblemen gave one another forks instead of toothpicks. I
wrote to Minello for a fresh consignment.

My shop — a good one, with pleasant living quarters — was in
the Italian part of London. I spoke Italian well enough; the
other merchants took me as one of themselves. I was abashed
to find how many of them were, like Minello, an example to us
priests in generosity and kindness. In their trading voyages
they took as many risks as we had ever taken for the Faith.
True, they did it for money, but not money that they would
ever have the leisure to enjoy. For the sake of their fat wives
and pretty *bambini*, they were prepared to founder in slippery

seas, or in the crevasses of the Alps. When we had thought of dying on the scaffold, we had at least been sure of spectators. The merchants' deaths might be unmarked, their graves unknown. And nobody would honour them as martyrs, though, perhaps, they had done more than we had to civilise mankind.

With these men and their families I went every Sunday to hear Mass where it was legal, at the chapel of the Portuguese ambassador. Here I formed a choir. It had the same success as in Rome; people packed the chapel and stood in the street outside, to hear our Catholic music. I was glad to be always busy, so that I went to bed weary. I dared not lie awake, because of my longing for Anne.

The Portuguese ambassador kept an English priest. To him I made my confession, admitting that I did not know whether I was myself still a priest. I had had no message from Rome. Yet Rome knew where to find me, since Robert Southwell did.

He came to see me in December, 1587. He stood in the shop, scowling at the forks, not speaking. I asked him what poems he had written lately. As if ashamed, he brought out one which, he said, he had written for Christmas.

As I in hoary winter's night
Stood shivering in the snow . . .

I thought this poem, *The Burning Babe* the most perfect I had yet seen in our language. When I said so, Robert snatched it out of my hands, and left me. I understood why. A man who could write like this could not endure that what he had written should remain unread. He must show it even to me, whom he despised. Now my praise made him despise himself.

It was not until the following July that he came to see me again.

"I suppose," he said abruptly, "that you're not willing to see Father Garnett."

"Why should you suppose that? Until I hear otherwise, Father Garnett is my superior. I've been awaiting his orders."

"You know very well he can't come into London."

"I did not know that."

"Well, he can't. The gates of the City are guarded night and day, because of all this panic about invasion. If you want to see him you'll have to go to Hampstead Heath."

"When?"

"Tomorrow evening. There's an alehouse called Jack Straw's Castle. Go and sit outside the alehouse until after sunset."

"Sunset's late, this time of year."

"I can't help that. We have to meet when the place has become deserted."

It was all of a piece with our Jesuit plotting that we should arrange to meet in a deserted place, and find it swarming with people. Robert ought to have foreseen this. He had known (though I had not) that Jack Straw's Castle was on the top of a hill. Every hilltop in England then was crowded with children collecting brushwood, with men piling it on a high frame, with women clutching tinder and flint, all ready to light a bonfire.

I gave my horse into the alehouse-keeper's charge, and sat watching the people. A gentleman rode up and they all gathered round him. "Everything's ready, sir." "There's a store of wood over here, sir." "We've built a shelter, sir, just as you said, to keep it dry."

This gentleman was the Justice of the Peace, without whose order the bonfire could not be lit. He stayed on horseback, never taking his eyes off the hills far away to the south. When the landlord brought him ale, he ordered a pint a head, for "all these honest people." The honest people cheered him.

Just after sunset I heard a jingling noise, coming out of the woods to the north. Six great horses were pulling a coach up a hill. Though it had no coat of arms, it was clearly the coach of a nobleman; outriders on fine horses, in livery sewn with silver, came before and after. As the coach drew up at the alehouse, the landlord was already bowing and smiling; and all the people hastened to see what great man had come to inspect their preparations. The J.P. dismounted and pushed through the crowd, so that he could be the first to bow before the Queen's emissary. Amid cries of "God save the Queen!" the door of the coach was opened, and a man very richly dressed appeared on the step. It was Father Garnett.

He was not in the least at a loss. He smiled at the J.P., and said: "All in order here?"

The J.P. proudly took him to inspect the bonfire. I heard Father Garnett say: "Your good service ought to be reported to Her Majesty."

Around me people were asking one another who this was. Too young for Lord Burleigh . . . Too old for Sir Walter Raleigh . . . And the Earl of Leicester was assembling his troops at Tilbury. This must, they decided, be Sir Francis Walsingham.

I felt someone tugging at my cloak. Out of the coach Robert's voice whispered: "Get in!"

So I did, while everyone else was watching Father Garnett. With a gesture full of grace and authority, he was telling the people what they knew already, that they had to keep a good look-out to the south. Such was the effect of a coach and six (with outriders) that they were hanging on his words.

"Fools!" muttered Robert.

There was a burst of cheering. Far away, on the hills of Surrey, a light had appeared. As if it were good news, the people cheered the signal which told them that forces never yet defeated were in sight of English land.

Father Garnett graciously gave his consent to the lighting of the bonfire. As it blazed up we heard from far away drums beating the alarm.

"To Tilbury!" said Father Garnett, sidling towards the coach.

The cries re-echoed round us: "To Tilbury!" Men were leaping (or lurching) into the saddle, those who had no horses were running, and everyone but the old men guarding the bonfire made off towards Hampstead village.

Father Garnett ordered his coachman to take another direction, westwards. After a few minutes we stopped, and Father Garnett got out, telling Robert and myself to follow.

We were still very high. We could see the beacon flaring up

on Harrow Hill, and even as we looked new points of light began to answer, away and away to the north. From Hampstead village we heard a fresh burst of cheering.

"Fools!" Robert said again.

"Oh, they are all drunk," said Father Garnett.

"No," I said. "They are a little drunk, but that's not the reason for their high spirits."

At this there was dead silence. Father Garnett briskly led the way, until we were out of earshot of his attendants. Then he went into a thicket, and stood with his back against a tree. He said to me: "Do you acknowledge me as your superior?"

I knelt at his feet.

"Then why," he asked, "have you not come to me for orders?"

"Robert said that I was not to. He said you would come to me."

"That was when you were in prison. Since your escape you have been to see everyone else. You have seen your mother, which was a direct act of disobedience."

I nodded, but said nothing. I was trying to recall that state of mind in which I had thought it right that I should be forbidden to see my parents.

"You have been to Wisbech Castle, and spent a long time talking to" — he spat the name out — "Christopher Bagshaw."

"Yes."

"Did you know that he was disputing the authority of Father Weston?"

"I did not know that Father Weston had any authority over him, or could have, not being a bishop."

"Father Weston is a member of our Society. You knew that?"

"Yes."

"And yet you made no attempt to see him?"

"I don't know Father Weston. I do know Christopher Bagshaw. I went to ask his forgiveness. When we were together in the Clink I refused to believe what he said about Father Parsons. Now I know it is all true."

"You know nothing of the kind."

"When I was in Rome—"

"When you were in Rome you had some crazy delusion, which led you to attack Father Parsons with a knife. You had to be restrained for your own good."

"If I am a madman, who attacks people with knives, how can you trust yourself in this lonely place with me? You know very well what the truth is. You hid in Arundel Castle, and heard the searchers calling you by name. They had been waiting for you in Newhaven—the very port where Parsons told you to land."

In his most majestic manner, Father Garnett said: "The searchers did not call us by our names."

"Then why did Robert tell me at the time—?"

"You misunderstood me!" Robert said.

I got up off my knees and faced them. "Have you blotted out the past, then, both of you? Are you so sure that the Spaniards are going to win?"

"We are not here to answer the Bloody Question," Father Garnett said. "That's your peculiar art. When Walsingham put the Bloody Question to you, you showed such cowardice—"

"Where's the cowardice? I told Walsingham what I thought. I said that Queen Mary and King Philip were good Catholics, and they fought against the Pope. I said English Catholics would do the same again."

"That is not a Catholic answer."

"Then what is? Are you conceding the Government's whole case—that a Catholic is the same thing as a traitor?"

"We are not bound," said Father Garnett, "to answer every question put to us by everybody."

"You're bound to answer that one, when it's put to you by poor persecuted English Catholics. They have to suffer and die for Parsons' treason."

"Your delusions about Father Parsons led you to commit the sin of disobedience."

"He had no power to order me to commit mortal sin."

"He was ordering you to make a retreat."

"He meant, once I was hidden from the world, to murder me. My consent would have been suicide."

"Can you prove that he intended any such thing?"

"Of course I can't. But it's reasonable to think so, since he delivered me into the hands of Walsingham."

"There is no need for these absurd excuses. We know that you are in fact a renegade. You have even had the effrontery to ask for a dispensation from your vows."

"If I were a renegade, I would never have troubled to ask. I would have gone over to the Protestants."

"What you have done is a worse betrayal."

"Why? I have asked the Pope to let me lead a good Catholic life, but as a layman."

"We have heard enough," said Father Garnett. "It is obvious what happened when you were in the Tower. You were spared further torture on condition that you would act as an agent for Walsingham."

"You think that's obvious? The people up there on the hill thought it obvious that you _were_ Walsingham."

Robert shouted into my face: "But you _are_—you _are_ a Government spy."

"If I were, I could have had you both arrested, up there, on the hill. You trusted in my silence. You trust it now."

Father Garnett waved this aside. "Whatever you may have intended, the effect of your actions has been to benefit Walsingham. Using the powers vested in me, I exclude you from the Society of Jesus."

He then pronounced this as a formal sentence, in Latin. I drank in the words. When he had finished, I said: "Then I'm no longer a Jesuit. But am I still a priest?"

Garnett retorted: "You have never been a priest. Your ordination was invalid. You lied about your age."

I was about to say that I had not, when the full glory of my freedom burst upon me. I said: "So I can fight for my country, like those villagers?"

"The right company for you!" said Garnett.

I went on: "And I suppose I am free to marry?"

Robert burst into tears. "What a disgusting idea!"

I went running back to Jack Straw's Castle, to fetch my horse. Then I rode down to Hampstead, and took the breastplate and helmet and arquebus handed out to me by torchlight. I rode with all the others to the gates of London. Nobody asked for my papers; it was enough that I was with my countrymen in arms.

Near my shop, I dropped out of the ranks, if ranks they could be called. The infantry, finding itself delayed in the narrow streets, had begun a country dance. I went home for some baggage. It may seem a strange thing to take to a war, but I could not go long without my hair dye. My own colouring would become apparent within two days.

Outside my shop stood a man-at-arms — a real one, not a morris-dancing villager. I cried out: "*Cosa c'è?*" and my Italian neighbours put their heads out of the windows. They told me that the Queen had sent men of her own bodyguard to protect all foreigners. She feared that the armed villagers might show their love of country by looting alien shops.

"What a great Queen she is!" my neighbours remarked. "To think of such a thing, at such a moment . . . I doubt if the Spaniards will take such good care of us."

They all took it for granted that the Spaniards would win, though they were careful to say so only in Italian. "Have you seen those peasants?" they asked me. "What do they think a war is, that they go to it dancing?"

When I said I was going to join them, they cried out in distress. "You will only be killed!"

One man said: "It is something, though, to die as they are going to die — as part of one united country. If only we in Italy . . ."

In the end my neighbours wished me well, and promised to keep an eye on my shop. I rode to Tilbury, where I soon took my place among other horsemen learning the arts of war. Yes, learning still, even at this last moment. My clumsiness with arms I had never handled before caused no surprise. I managed my horse better than a good many others.

I saw, but did not hear, the famous speech of the Queen. The ranks drawn up for her close inspection were those of men who had actually done some fighting. We beginners were stationed farther off. But in the end she did ride near us too, and I saw her face — the face of a woman fifty-five years old, pale and haggard, framed in someone else's hair. Something in it showed me what I had never understood before. Her speech (which was printed, and handed out to us the next day) mentioned the warnings that she had received of her own danger. I knew them to be well founded. The Babington plot had been a real plot; and yet she rode among us now almost unguarded. When she caught my eye I felt at once that nobody could kill her. She had signed the death warrant of Campion and many others; and I myself could not have been tortured without her express permission. These were things I knew, but could not feel when her smile beamed upon me. Like the ten thousand men around me, I could only bless her name.

The following Sunday, I was amazed to see how many of those present did as I did, and moved quietly out of the way of the Protestant service, which was held in the open air. I joined the followers of the Catholic Lord Montague, who had many times protested in the House of Lords against the treatment of us priests. Now he was here with his son, his grandson, his tenants and his servants. When we had moved out of earshot of the Protestants, an old priest said Mass for the victory of England.

Afterwards, as I rode back to the camp, I recognised one of the men coming away from the Protestant service. I said: "Good morning, Nick."

Despite my black beard, he knew me. "You see," he whispered, "I'm not a real deserter."

"Nor a real Puritan," I said. "You've been to church."

"Well, sir, it was Dr. Sharp who preached, and he is worth hearing. He told us about this Don Pedro they've captured at sea. The Spanish chief of staff. It seems Lord Burleigh asked him what the Spaniards intended to do. Don Pedro said:

"Subdue your nation, and root you all out." And then they asked him what he meant to do with English Catholics. He said: "As they're good men, we'll send them directly to Heaven, while we send you heretics to Hell."

Two years before, I would have thought this was one of Walsingham's fables. Now I thought it was quite likely true. I said to Nick: "Who knows — we may go to Heaven together."

He answered cheerfully: "Yes, I hope it'll be Heaven." And then just as cheerfully, but in a whisper: "We're none of us much longer for this world. I know what it is to fight against the Spanish army."

I told him the thought which had been some consolation to me. "When the Government cut off the Scottish Queen's head, they knew it would mean war with Spain. They must have reckoned they could win."

"Ah! Our generals might reckon so. But if you'd done any fighting, sir, you'd know how often the generals are wrong."

I looked across Tilbury marsh to the bridge of boats, which connected our camp with Gravesend. One Spanish galley could ram it. I looked at Tilbury Fort, and wondered how long it would hinder the Prince of Parma, who had never lost a pitched battle.

I looked at the great elm trees which overhung our camp. They were so clear in the sunshine, I could have counted the leaves. Would I have them to look at as I died? Would I have another vision of Anne's face?

Some two miles away, in a boat-builder's yard by the river, they were boiling pitch. If I could do nothing else before I died, I could fill my nostrils with a hot incomparable smell. I rode across the marsh to the river bank.

So I was one of the first to see the messenger coming from Kent, across the bridge of boats. He was covered with dust, and riding so fast that the planks went swaying, and the boats pitched as if to throw him into the river.

He was across, and safe. And we were safe. Our ships had scattered the Armada. However good the Spanish army was, it could not reach us. Our army was disbanded a few days later.

XVI

THIS TIME I HAD to pay a larger bribe to see Christopher Bagshaw.

"Things are harder for all of us now," he whispered. "It's the Jesuits' fault; they said Mass for the success of the Armada."

I whispered back: "That's why I came to see you. The news of these Masses is all over London. They were said even inside the Tower; the Earl of Arundel ordered them."

"He would; he's under Jesuit direction. Robert Southwell's direction . . . Is Robert still free?"

"Yes, but because of those Masses, they've begun to execute priests again."

Christopher groaned. "Not only because of that. The worst thing was the pamphlet."

"What? Has Parsons written another pamphlet?"

"It had Allen's name on it. It was to be given out in England, when the Spaniards landed. When they were defeated every copy was destroyed — except, of course, the copies already in Walsingham's hands. This pamphlet said that Pope Sixtus had issued another Bull against the Queen."

"Oh, God."

"Elizabeth sent men to read it to us. It describes her as 'a bastard, conceived and born by incestuous adultery'."

"Incestuous?"

"There's an old story—haven't you heard it?—that Anne Boleyn was really King Henry's daughter. All nonsense, of course, unless Henry seduced Lady Boleyn when he was ten years old. But Parsons is fond of the story. Well, when they read it to us, they asked us if we were going to obey this Bull. We seculars all said no."

"And the Jesuits?"

"They said the whole thing was a forgery. Now the odd thing is, they're right. Parsons and Allen forged it. They'd failed in all their efforts to persuade the Pope that he ought to issue such a Bull. So they pretended he had issued it. You know, Paul, I don't think the Pope is going to forgive them for that."

"Then perhaps the Pope will do something . . . But Christopher, until he does, oughtn't we to do something? Parsons' lies are destroying innocent people. There's a poor girl been executed for doing what Anne did—helping a priest to escape. Shouldn't we tell someone in authority the difference between ourselves and the Jesuits?"

Christopher sighed. "I've thought of this often, but . . . Suppose they say, if we're as loyal as we pretend, we'll tell them where to find Robert Southwell. Would you do that?"

"No."

"You see? And even if we did make up our minds to talk to Protestants—where would we find a civilised one, with brains? Mr. Gray, sitting watching us over there—would you talk to him?" He laughed. "Do you know what you said, Paul? 'The difference between ourselves and the Jesuits.' As if you weren't a Jesuit."

"No more I am." I told him about the scene on Hampstead Heath.

"That sounds a rough-and-ready ceremony. Perhaps

Garnett had the power to exclude you from the Society of Jesus. But to tell you that you'd never been a priest — "

"I hope to God he's right."

"Why? Oh, that girl . . . She was here the other day. She looks different now. Such a hard face!"

"Hard? My little Anne?"

"Well, sour, you know, with her mouth pulled down at the corners."

"What can have happened to her? What have those cruel devils in York been doing? Did she tell you — "

"She said hardly anything to me. I suppose Weston told her not to."

"Weston? The Jesuit? Why should she listen to him?"

"He has a great reputation," Christopher said, "for casting out evil spirits. Anne has a little brother called Harry, and she thinks he's possessed by a devil."

"Oh, yes — he screams at night."

"He's a handful in the daytime too. Anne brought him here to see if Weston could quieten him down. Which he did. Tying him up in wet sheets, burning sulphur under his nose . . . I suppose the child was frightened out of his wits."

"But Anne . . . Didn't she have any news at all?"

"You must ask her yourself." Christopher's voice trembled. "It breaks my heart to lose you, Paul. If you'd been still a priest, you could have done so much! Now that the Spaniards are defeated, we'd be listened to in Rome. But who's free to go there? Only John Mush, and you."

"I must go to Anne."

When I reached my parents' house I understood, from the servants' haste to make me comfortable, that the whole household knew me. My parents made light of the danger. "Even the Council of the North," my mother said, "has never punished a woman for sheltering her own son."

I told them everything. "I am so glad!" my father said. "It's all over Yorkshire — this tale of the Jesuits saying Mass for the Armada. I could not bear to think that you had any part in that."

"And yet it's a sad thing for you," said my mother, "to be told you're not a priest."

"It may be a very happy thing, if Anne Clitheroe will marry me."

They looked at each other. My father shook his head. I asked him why. It was my mother who found the words.

"There's been such a change in that girl! I swear to you, Paul, I can scarcely get a civil word out of her now. I know it's partly the boy. The child's mad, and he's driving her mad; I make allowance for that. And her dad forever grumbling . . . And her sister's disgrace . . . But, as I told her, that girl was only a child, poor thing! And there's no call for Anne to scold her other sisters, if they so much as say good evening to a man. It makes her sound a shrew, and so I tell her. That is — I used to tell her. Not now. Since Anne came back from Wisbech, I'm not welcome in that house."

"Why not?"

"Paul — I don't know. I don't know. When we were in London, she was like my own daughter. I swear I've never changed to her. Why she's changed to me . . ." My mother was weeping, and for a moment I felt her anguish more than my own.

I could do nothing that night; the gates of York were closed. But at first light I went to the stable for my horse. I rode into York, showing my false papers, and asking for the house of the Lord Mayor. Then I turned aside into the Shambles.

While I was wondering which house it could be, I saw a big red-faced man opening up a shop, and I knew at once that this was Mr. Clitheroe. I must have seen him when I was a child.

He looked suspiciously at me when I asked for Anne. "What for?" he said. "Who are you?"

I said: "I am a silver merchant from London. My business is doing well, and I want to marry your daughter."

Immediately he was on my side. He led me into his best room, and called Anne. When she replied that she was busy in the kitchen, he sternly told her sisters to do the work. There was a grating, screeching noise from the mad child. Somebody slammed a door on that. At last Anne came into the room. When she saw me she tried to run out again, but her father pushed her back, and shut us in together.

She would not look at me, and she shuddered away from my touch. "Why did you come?" she moaned. "I was just beginning to be at peace in my mind."

"At peace?" I said. "Without me?"

"What you want is wicked."

"No! I'm free to marry you now."

"You mean — because you've been unfrocked?"

"Not unfrocked, Anne. That wouldn't set me free to marry. But it seems I wasn't properly ordained. I've never been a priest."

"Then you've been deceiving everybody. Father Weston said you had. He said you were unfrocked — or turned out of the Society of Jesus; I thought that was the same thing — because you were a deceiver and a villain."

"What did he say I had done?"

"You spy on the good priests. You make reports to Walsingham."

"Oh, Anne! You know I was put on the rack, because I wouldn't tell Walsingham even the names of two smugglers who tried to rob me. Is it likely I would tell him anything about my friends?"

"Father Weston said that showed your cunning. You were put on the rack just for a little while, and after that people trusted you."

"Why should you take Weston's word for that?"

"Because Father Weston's good! I know he is! He cast the devils out of Harry."

The grating, screeching noise began again, just outside. Anne made to open the door, but I held her back. She cried out: "I must go to Harry! Nobody else can do anything with him."

"There's your proof, then!" I shouted. "Father Weston's a fraud; he never cast any devils out of the child."

"He did, he did! Only they've come back since."

I heard the noise as Mr. Clitheroe hit the child, and dragged him away from the door. And still I held Anne in my merciless arms. I said: "How could you even listen to such nonsense? The Jesuits are against me for one reason. They wanted the Spaniards to win."

Anne cried out: "I wanted the Spaniards to win!"

I dropped my arms and let her stagger back against the door. The look I gave her daunted her a moment, but then she burst out: "Why not? The Spaniards would have brought some justice."

I said: "They would have brought looting and rape and murder."

"That's what I mean by justice! It would have served these people right, for what they've done to us. Do you know, it's Harry — little Harry — they point at now in the street. They say: 'Like mother, like son.' They say she must have been mad, to do what she did."

"Anne! Don't lose yourself in dreams of revenge! You're the girl who went into the worst prisons, and talked to the worst people, and never lost your Christian charity."

"That was easy. I was going as a nun goes — from a calm peaceful place."

"The Foscues told me it was you who made their home so peaceful."

"Did they say that? They can't have known me. You don't really know me. We all behave better with strangers. But with my own family . . . With all these neighbours, and their ugliness and spite . . . I'll never be calm here. When my brothers and sisters are old enough to be left, I don't care what the danger is — I'll go to France and be a nun."

"Don't say that, Anne! Don't do what you have no vocation to do. Look what I've suffered through making that mistake! Marry me — then you can do as many good works as any nun. You can visit prisons every day if you like. We'll have enough servants — "

"God be praised! What you say doesn't even tempt me.

Because I feel it through and through — that you're a wicked man. I know that from my own experience."

"Anne! What wrong have I done you?"

"The worst wrong of all — confusing me in my faith. You said it wasn't mortal sin for me to go to church. And your mother said the same. I can't bear to look at her, because of that."

"If it was mortal sin, you've made up for it by now. Why should you go on and on tormenting yourself?"

"Because it torments me ten times worse to be told that my mother chose to die for nothing."

"Your mother didn't choose to die. She felt sure of being found guilty at her trial. The only choice before her was the manner of her death."

"You don't know," Anne sobbed, "you don't know what that wicked old man said. Her stepfather — the Lord Mayor, he was then — told her that the whole case would be dropped, if she'd only go to church. My mother could have lived. She could have saved us all this misery, stopped the apprentice from seducing my sister, kept Harry in his right mind (because he was a dear little boy, before) held everything in order as it used to be, if she had gone to church. And so it must be mortal sin to go to church. It must matter more than husband or children or home. I can't think otherwise — I can't!"

That was the end. I tried to kiss and caress her. But it was too late; her mind had so worked on her body that she shrank away from me, as from a toad. A year before, I know, she had felt otherwise. What I shall never know is — if I had embraced her then, trampling on her scruples and my own, would I have brought her to such ecstasy that she would have thought me right in everything? That question troubles me still; at the time it almost made me mad. I went back to London ready to give up my shop, my business and perhaps my life.

Then John Mush came to me for shelter. He showed me how useful my shop could be, as a refuge and meeting-place for those priests who thought as we did. For their sake I kept up my disguise, and I was not arrested until some three years afterwards.

At the time I thought this arrest my own fault. A few days before it, a man swathed in sables came into my shop. While he examined the best of my forks, he hummed a tune. I had last heard it from the Russian ambassador, Molvaninov.

I could not resist asking this Englishman how he came to know a Russian song. He explained that he had been our ambassador in Russia, and still could scarcely believe that he was alive. He told me that the heir to the Russian throne, the child Dmitri, had been murdered, with the people of a whole town as eye-witnesses. Everybody knew the murderers as agents of Boris Godunov, whom nobody dared to accuse.

As my customer talked I was entranced. I could not hear enough of this wild country, where I had dreamed of spending all my life. I asked him whether he had been there when Father Possevino visited Tsar Ivan. He said he had.

"Possevino wasn't a bad fellow. I went to see him once, about some Venetian prisoners . . ."

In his talk he used Russian words, and I let him see I understood them. I forgot to invent a reason why.

After my arrest I thought it must have been this man who denounced me. I was wrong. Months later the Protestant Bishop of London showed me the letter of denunciation. There was no signature, but I knew the writing as Father Garnett's.

I did not say so. But I looked at this Protestant bishop, and saw that he was a new kind of interrogator. He did not threaten me with rack or scaffold; he did not urge me to betray my friends. He seemed even to respect my faith. Only he asked me gently whether I knew how closely this faith had become entangled with treason.

At this I explained to him the difference between the two kinds of Catholics. I said that if Her Majesty would make a show of banishing Christopher Bagshaw and certain others, and would ship them over the Channel, they would then be able to appeal to the Pope.

This, after some time, was done. One of the things my friends discovered, during their long, intricate appeals, was that Garnett had been wrong. I had been properly ordained. Parsons had put about the story that I was not, in order to prevent the Papal Courts from considering my affidavit. This, and all my documents, had long since disappeared. I was, though not a Jesuit, still a priest.

I accepted this without further dispute. Since I had been deceived in Anne, how could I want to marry anyone? I did want very much to help my friends in Rome. During one of our appeals, I heard Parsons tell the Pope that the defeat of the Armada was a mere temporary setback. The Jesuits, being right, could not for long be defeated in any country. In Russia they had converted "the rightful Tsar, Dmitri, mistakenly thought to be murdered", and were following his victorious army to Moscow.

Now, in old age – for I never was worthy of martyrdom, and seem likely to die in bed – I mourn for my companions. I mourn for Robert Southwell, equivocator, martyr, a matchless poet lost. I mourn for Henry Garnett, put to death for his part in the Gunpowder Plot. I mourn for Molvaninov and countless Russians beside, who fell in the wars brought about by the Jesuits' favoured impostor. I mourn even for Christopher, John and myself, although we did survive to see the Pope rebuke Parsons, and put the leadership of English Catholics into better hands. The struggle dragged out over so many years, and undermined the faith of so many people, that we could feel no triumph when we won. Thinking of that struggle now, I remember that it made Anne's gentle face hard and bitter. I imagine her growing old within convent walls, as I have grown old immured in half-unwilling priesthood.

I have not been happy, and will not be on earth. I have done what I had, perhaps, no vocation to do. Yet I do it still, because it must be done, if we are ever to achieve unpersecuted, unpersecuting Faith.